Vampire Delights on Polar Nights

Jude Stephens

WCP

World Castle Publishing, LLC
Pensacola, Florida

Copyright © Jude Stephens 2010
Print ISBN: 9781629891323
eBook ISBN: 9781629891330
Second Edition World Castle Publishing, LLC, August 15, 2014
http://www.worldcastlepublishing.com

Licensing Notes

Cover: Karen Fuller
Editor: Maxine Bringenberg

Chapter 1

The wind was blowing hard from the northeast. Drifts of snow crept up the sides of the plain grey structure. Stark black letters stood out on the side of the building, letting everyone know that this was the Global Seed Vault. The building, less than 620 miles from the North Pole, had been dedicated a year before as scientists and researchers from all over the world looked on. The island, named Spitsbergen, was part of the Svalbard Archipelago.

On that day representatives from all over the world had ceremoniously carried in their precious seeds that would guarantee the world crop continuation in the event of any man made or natural disaster. After the last of the seeds were carried in and carefully stored, the people left the island. There was no need to have anyone maintain the seed vault. All monitoring was done remotely.

The helicopter now came in close to the grey structure, the whirling blades blowing snow high into the air as it gracefully landed.

Karen opened the door and took a look at the dismal grey structure that was going to be her new home for the next several months. She suppressed a shiver as she stepped out. Even though she was wearing a thermal snowsuit, she could feel the subzero temperature. Karen, a commander for the United Global Agency, or UGA — an agency that no one knew about, which was overseen by visionaries from many different countries — was anxious to begin this assignment. The agency looked after the future of Earth. It took care of things that needed taken care of, and it outranked kings, presidents, congresses, and parliaments.

The pilot came around from the other side of the chopper and pointed towards the door. Not able to hear over the loud whistle of the wind, Karen understood he wanted her to go ahead while he unloaded supplies from the chopper.

She made her way to the door and waited. The door opened with a hydraulic wheeze. Lowering the hood of her snowsuit, she removed her hat and goggles and turned at the sound of footsteps.

"Commander, welcome to Spitsbergen."

"Thank you, Bryce."

Karen was less than pleased to have Bryce as her second in command on this assignment. He was a typical male chauvinist who thought women were only put on this earth to worship at the altar of Bryce. Not that he had a problem getting women to do just that. Karen had to admit that he was good looking with his short military haircut, blue eyes, and a chiseled body that filled out his fatigues in all the right places.

Knowing she had to keep the upper hand with Bryce, she said, "I can find my way. Why don't you help Vaughn with the supplies?"

Without waiting for a response, she turned and started down the long hallway. She knew from looking at blueprints of the building that the hall led to a tunnel, which eventually sloped down 420 feet to where seeds were stored on either side in icy vaults. Karen came to the end of the tunnel and, pushing an unremarkable plate on the wall, waited while the hum of another hydraulic system began its work.

The wall slid open and she stepped forward, and with another hum the door closed and the elevator began its descent. Karen wondered what the good people of The Global Seed project would think of the little addition that was added on to their doomsday project.

This second level was another 620 feet below the first and was only accessible through this elevator. No one but UGA knew of its existence. Construction of the seed vault had been done using UGA contractors, who just happened to win the bid on the Seed Vault Project.

When the elevator finally came to a stop Karen stepped out and got her first look at a vampire.

Chapter 2

Karen wasn't aware that she held her breath. The specimen was magnificent. He was at least six feet tall, with broad shoulders and dark hair that curled at the collar of his plain white shirt. His jean clad thighs were massive, and Karen wondered what it would be like to straddle a strong thigh and.... She shook her head to clear it.

He was handcuffed and being escorted by two burly guards with tranquilizer guns. As they passed close by the vampire turned, and Karen sucked in her breath at the look in his bright blue eyes. His eyes blazed with hatred. If looks could kill, she would be a dead woman. She took a step back.

"Don't worry about him, Commander. He won't hurt you. The guards have enough fentanyl citrate in those tranqs to stop an elephant. My name is William Stutter; I'm the senior medical advisor here."

She shook his hand absently, staring at the rather nice backside of the retreating vampire. Rarely in her almost forty years of living had she seen such a handsome man. Though, she guessed that was incorrect. He wasn't a man, he was a vampire.

Recovering, she turned her attention back to Mr. Stutter, who looked like a strong wind could blow him over. He was short and thin with glasses perched on the end of his nose. His eyes, however, showed the intelligence that he had no doubt learned at an Ivy League school.

"Is everything in order? We only have a few days until the polar nights are upon us."

She wasn't looking forward to the polar nights. It unsettled her to think about the upcoming three and a half months of darkness that would descend upon them soon.

"Yes, Commander. The supplies are all in order and the...the required personnel will be arriving tomorrow."

Karen raised her eyebrows at the term "required personnel." More like sacrificial lambs, she thought to herself. She wasn't happy to be in command of this operation, but she had worked and believed in the UGA for the last twenty years and she always did her duty.

She spared Mr. Stutter a few more minutes and then asked to be taken to her quarters so that she could change and get down to business.

Once in her quarters, she showered and changed into her working clothes, plain khaki pants and a blue button up shirt. She swept her brown hair up into a haphazard bun and took a quick look in the mirror. She had never been one to waste her time on hair and makeup, and since the death of her husband three years ago, she hardly even gave it a thought. She turned so she could look at her ass in the mirror and sighed. It seemed that it expanded a little more everyday. She reminded herself she wasn't in bad shape for her age, and it really didn't matter anymore without Charlie.

She missed her husband. They had both worked for UGA and were married five years before he was killed in an airplane crash while on assignment in South America.

Leaving her quarters she made her way to the lab. Once there, she sought out Bryce in his office.

"I would like to see the files for all of the vampires and have the one who calls himself their leader brought to my office."

Bryce stood. "I don't know if that's a good idea, Commander."

"Has he shown overly aggressive behavior tendencies?"

"No, but...."

"Then please just do as I ask Bryce."

Karen almost felt sorry for the asshole. Until today, he had been in command of the seed vault, but with the critical time almost upon them, he had been replaced due to his lack of progress and the disaster that occurred last year.

"Suit yourself, Commander. Just be careful. He's a very good looking man, and I know it's been a while since you had one of those." Bryce turned and walked out.

Sonofabitch! Karen knew that he'd never liked her. He had a problem with any woman in a position of authority. She had heard his opinions of women over the years. "Women are only good for one thing"; "Women don't belong in the UGA." Karen wished she could fire his Archie Bunker ass, but he had connections to some folks in high places. Hell, maybe it had been a while since she was with a man, but it wasn't like she was a teenager with raging hormones. She hadn't really given sex too much thought since her husband died.

A clerk entered and with a slight nod handed her the files she'd requested. She sat down, anxious to learn about the vampires that were being kept here. The discovery of vampires had occurred thirty years earlier with the capture of one such creature in Edinburgh. Fortunately, the lead investigator on the case was a member of UGA. The vampire was quickly transferred to a UGA facility operating in England. Several of UGA's top scientists studied the vampire until it succumbed. The cause of death was unknown.

All was not in vain though. They learned that vampires indeed were susceptible to daylight. Also, the myths were true, and they did need blood to survive. Their sense of smell and sight were excellent, and they appeared to be stronger than normal men, but not Superman strong as usually portrayed in the movies.

Armed with the knowledge of vampires' existence, UGA had set up a task force to deal with them. It was, after all, the job of the agency to protect mankind. Over the years a few more were captured and kept in various UGA locations throughout the world.

In the last few years however, there had been more vampires captured than in the entire past thirty years, and the agency decided that a facility needed to be set up to deal with this new threat. Currently, there were eight vampires residing in a lab underneath the seed vault.

Karen had just opened the first file when there was a knock at her door.

"Come in," she called without looking up.

Hearing the door open and close, she finally looked up from her file.

Karen forgot how to breathe. The tall, handsome vampire that she had seen a few hours ago stood in front of her. Up close he was breathtaking. He had a long aquiline nose and his bright blue eyes were framed by long, thick lashes. Even though his hands were shackled, he stood tall and proud with a defiant gleam in his eye. He stared hard at her until she shifted her eyes away from the fierceness of his gaze.

"Please have a seat, um…Mr…."

The vampire said nothing, but sat down in the chair in front of the desk. Since he wasn't forthcoming, Karen shuffled through the files on her desk.

"Yes…here we are. Mr. Nicholas Patroclus. It says here that you were discovered in Greece six months ago. You've had no infractions since your stay with us."

"Stay?"

Karen's head snapped up at the sound of his voice. It sent a shiver down her spine. His voice was low and soft, but with an unmistakable authority.

"I am being held here against my will."

"Well, yes, but it has not been determined what kind of threat you are to the world's population, Mr. Patroclus. You have been the first of your kind to even communicate with us. All we want to do is study your species."

"Study? It's my understanding that last year you let five of my kind die during the polar nights."

A look of sorrow passed over Karen's face. She'd read the report. Last year during the three and a half month long polar nights, the five vampires kept here had unexplainably perished.

"We didn't mean for them to die. We had no idea what they needed because they didn't tell us. Now that you have stepped forward and let us know of your special needs, we are going to help you. That is why I am here."

The vampire's eyebrows rose as he regarded the woman before him.

"Will you be taking care of all of us yourself?"

It took her a few seconds to understand.

"Oh no...I mean I'm here to oversee operations. We have some additional personnel coming in to do the actual...um...work."

"Work?"

Karen was getting tired of his repeating everything she said as a question.

"Yes, work. We are looking at this as just another assignment regardless of the unique situation. You have guaranteed that you will provide us with information, and I guarantee that I will deliver you women who will provide the release you need to survive the polar nights."

The vampire stared at her with an intensity that began to make her nervous. She wasn't sure if it was because he was a vampire or because he was as handsome as a Greek god. Karen couldn't help but stare at his mouth. His lips were full and filled with the promise of soft, slow kisses and many other delights. Letting her eyes travel downward, she noticed how his broad chest was well defined by the white shirt he wore. From the little bit she could see, his skin beneath the shirt was smooth and golden. Involuntarily, she licked her lips. The movement drew his attention to her mouth.

"I would be more than happy to 'work' with you."

Karen imagined "working" with him. She just knew his body would be hard…everywhere. She wondered how old he was…how many women he had "worked" with. She instinctively knew that he would have the ability to make a woman come apart in his arms.

As if sensing her thoughts, he leaned forward until he was inches from her and breathed in.

"I smell your excitement, and I bet if I were to touch you, I would feel the juices of your desire dripping from your sex."

Karen couldn't breathe. She felt her body tingling and pulsating from a place deep inside of her, and yes, she felt the dampness seep from between her thighs. She wasn't aware she had gotten up and was now standing in front of him. She placed a hand on his chest and it was as she imagined. Rock hard.

He stood and backed her up until her bottom was on the edge of the desk. He pushed her legs apart and moved in close so the huge bulge in his jeans was up against her core. The material of her khaki pants was thin, and she could feel his cock pulsating against her. Without a thought she began to move her hips up and down, causing a sweet friction against her throbbing clit.

She heard him moan. "Yes...that's it. Let go. Use my body to find your release. It's been a long time since you've allowed yourself to come, hasn't it?"

Karen increased the pressure, grinding her clit harder against his cock until she felt the first wave of her muscles contracting.

The vampire lifted his arms over her head to encircle her so she wouldn't fall backwards while the orgasm ripped through her. With his cock still pushed against her, he leaned down and whispered against her mouth. "I need to fuck you. Will you allow it?"

For a split second she froze and then recoiled. "Let me up."

He immediately lifted his arms.

Karen felt her cheeks burn red with her humiliation. She had never done anything like that in her entire life. Trying to get herself together, she said, "I apologize, Mr. Patroclus. I don't know what came over me. I can assure you that from now on I will act with the utmost professionalism. You also have my assurance that you and your companions will have women here tomorrow night as the polar nights begin. These specially selected women are ready and willing to satisfy your needs."

Before he could speak she rang a buzzer that summoned the guard to take Nicholas back to his room. She spared him a quick glance and recoiled at the heat in his gaze.

Chapter 3

Nicholas walked back to his quarters in bewilderment, his mind picturing how she had used his body to find her release. He didn't know the woman's name, only that she was in charge here, and that he had to have her. This more than anything puzzled Nicholas. She wasn't the type of woman he usually found attractive. Hell, she was pretty enough, but she was older than the twenty-something women he usually took to his bed. But when he'd held her in his arms, he felt a longing that he was unfamiliar with. A need arose within him, and he knew without a doubt that he needed to be inside her.

As soon as the guard retreated after depositing him behind the locked and heavily guarded door, he was surrounded by the other vampires.

"Well, Amigo, how did it go?"

Nicholas looked at Eduardo, a vampire captured in Buenos Aires last month. He didn't want to go into the more intimate details of his meeting with the new commander.

"It's going according to plan. They will be bringing the women to us tomorrow night. It will be upon each of us to do our job once they are given to us."

"I'll have no trouble doing my job. I've been in this hole for two months now. I've never gone so long without a woman."

Nicholas shot Blayze a warning look when he saw Soren's eyes narrow at Blayze's words. The two had not gotten along very well. Nicholas had to admit Blayze was a bit annoying at times. He was too snooty even for a Frenchman, let alone for some of the rugged vampires in the room. Nicholas worried more about Soren than any of the other vampires here. He was angry. Soren had been in captivity the longest, almost ten months. Nicholas was afraid that Soren wouldn't be able to follow through with their plan.

He was aware that Soren didn't agree with his plan to use the women to aid in their eventual escape. Soren didn't think that Nicholas should be talking to their captors at all. Nicholas agreed. It went against the code for a vampire to communicate information to a captor, but Nicholas knew they were running out of time. They would not survive the three and a half months of darkness that accompanied the polar nights in the Antarctic. No one knew this better than Soren.

Soren had lost his brother in this hell hole last year. That was how he'd been caught. He'd tracked his brother to this place, but he was too late. He hadn't survived the polar nights. Nicholas almost laughed at the irony of the whole situation. Vampires were creatures of the night…except when night lasted more than a month. Their bodies need to shut down to regenerate with the blood they took in. When faced with prolonged night, their organs didn't maximize the blood and quickly began to deteriorate.

The other seven vampires looked to Nicholas to save them. It fell on his shoulders, as he was the oldest vampire among them. He had thought long and hard of a way to escape before the polar nights began. He honestly didn't think his captors would agree to bring in women to have sex with the vampires. He was a little shocked that they'd bought his lies. This was the best plan he could come up with and they now had no choice. They needed to lure the women into helping them escape.

"I suggest that you enjoy the last day of sun, my brothers. We will need our strength and resolve for the task ahead of us."

The vampires began walking back to their rooms, with the exception of Soren.

"Will you be able to handle this, Soren?"

Nicholas was worried that Soren wouldn't be able to feign passion for the woman he would need to seduce. The other vampires were eager for this assignment. They basically would fuck anything that moved.

"Don't worry about me. I will do what I have to do to get out of here, but when the time is right I will kill anyone involved with UGA." He stood to leave. "And that includes the whore who is willing to fuck a vampire in the name of science."

Nicholas watched him leave. He understood his hatred. Nicholas had spent many hundreds of years living with hatred, and had lost most of his emotions years ago. He couldn't feel any sympathy for the woman that was to be given to Soren.

His mind briefly thought about the commander and the interlude they'd had earlier. He was still puzzled by his body's reaction to her. He shook his head, shrugging it off as not having had a woman in all the time he had been there. Well, tomorrow would take care of that. He would be given his own woman to seduce and use. He smiled at the thought.

Chapter 4

Karen slowly made her way to the common room where the newly arrived women were gathered, awaiting her arrival. She was to debrief them and make them comfortable. Well, as comfortable as could be expected when their assignment was to have sexual intercourse with a different species.

The eight women awaiting her were very well known to her, even though she hadn't personally met any of them. She had read their files, as they were all UGA employees. She knew why each one of them had volunteered for this assignment. Their ages ran from twenty-five to forty, and they were all attractive, intelligent women with their own reasons for being there. Some were alone in the world, others had lost their husbands. A couple of them had a vivacious appetite for life and took every opportunity to live it to the fullest. And one had nothing to lose. Tears came to Karen's eyes as she thought about that particular woman. Karen admired and respected each of them, and it was her job to make sure that they got whatever it was they had come here for.

Karen opened the door and the women who had been chatting and having a glass of wine became quiet.

"Hello, my name is Karen Walls and I'm the commander in charge of this facility. I want to personally thank each of you for your sacrifice and dedication to UGA. Because of our organization, nuclear strikes have been avoided, assassinations preempted, and destruction of lands stopped. We do this not for the glory but for mankind, so that generations may continue to enjoy this earth as we have.

"Now you stand here ready to take on a possible new threat. We've known about the existence of vampires for the last thirty years. Until now, communication was non-existent. We hope to be able to find out more information from these vampires, but there is an outside threat that we need to overcome. The polar nights have proven to be lethal to the vampires unless they have sexual release. It was explained to us that their urge for sexual activity increases the longer they don't fall under their death sleep, and if denied it will eventually begin to shut down their organs until they succumb."

A woman stepped forward from the quiet crowd.

"Why don't you just move the vampires to another location where there are no polar nights?"

The other women murmured their agreement with the woman's question.

"That's a good question. We thought about doing that. We even tried to find another facility that would be secure. But as you know, this information was only given to us a few days ago, and by then it was too late to start a transfer which would be costly. Plus the possibility of an escape would be elevated. This was our only option."

Another woman stepped forward.

"I volunteered for this assignment, and I fully understand the dangers, but have you taken any measures to assure our safety?"

Karen could understand their fear. Fear came with any assignment one took when working in the UGA. Any decent agent would want to minimize any potential risks.

"We have taken some precautionary measures. All of the vampires are being given a drug in their daily dose of blood that weakens them so they do not have their usual superior strength."

One of the woman shouted, "Well hells bells, how are they going to get their fuck on if they don't have their usual strength?"

Most of the women laughed.

"We've been assured by our scientists that it will not affect their libido. We made them promise that all sexual activity will be consensual. No one will be asked to do anything out of their comfort zone. One last thing, we installed a secret panic button in every bathroom. So if there is something going down that threatens you, get to the bathroom and press the button. Armed guards will be there in seconds."

Karen looked around and the women seemed satisfied with the precautions taken on their behalf.

"Now, even though we all may know each other a bit, why don't we introduce ourselves before the vampires arrive?"

A tall, blonde woman stepped forward. Athletic and wholesome, she was well built with a bit of muscle. Karen was sure this girl went to the gym everyday.

"Hi. My name is Tamika," she said sweetly.

Another woman stood, this one petite with straight long black hair. She was quite beautiful and obviously of Asian descent. One couldn't help notice that she was abundantly endowed topside.

"Hi, my name is Juls, and yes, they are real." She sat back down as laughter broke out.

Next, a woman with curly light brown hair moved forward. She was pretty, with a twinkle in her big brown eyes. Just by looking at her, one could tell she was easy going and lighthearted and had a zest for life.

"My name is Nette, and if there is a cowboy vampire back there, he is mine!" She said with a slight southern accent.

All of the women smiled at her, which was most likely the reaction she always got from people. She exuded warmth and charm.

A redheaded woman was next to stand. She smiled sweetly but looked a little nervous. Karen was sure that it wasn't just the unusual assignment that she had signed up for making her nervous. It seemed as if she was not comfortable with new people.

"My name is Barbara," she said quickly, and sat down again.

Next, a tall, dark haired woman came forward. She had the polished look of a socialite: thin and immaculately dressed and coifed.

"Hello. My name is Diane. I'm pleased to meet you."

A petite woman with long brown hair stood up, and Karen bet that she was the envy of every woman in the room. She had sexy curves in all the right places.

"Hey everyone, my name is Samantha."

There were two women left, a blonde bombshell that looked like a supermodel, and a girl that Karen knew was twenty-five years old but looked like no more than seventeen. She was thin and wore glasses.

The supermodel stood and said, "Hi, I'm Holly," and with a toss of her long hair sat down again.

The young woman stood, and without meeting anyone's gaze said, "I'm Sparkle."

Karen smiled at her. "What a very pretty and unusual name."

Sparkle smiled back.

"Well then, it's nice to meet you all. Ah, here come the men. Again, the UGA thanks you for your sacrifice and your dedication to our cause."

She watched as the women braced themselves to become intimately acquainted with a vampire.

Chapter 5

The vampires entered the room led by Nicholas. Each of them carried themselves with cool confidence, no doubt having seduced many women over their long lives.

Nicholas perused the room of women and nodded to the men to proceed. He spotted the commander off to the side, and as if she felt his gaze on her, she looked over to him. Her cheeks flushed with color, and she quickly looked away.

Nicholas stood back and let the men mingle. It mattered not to him who ended up in his bed. These women were a means to an end and nothing else.

He felt a slight touch on his arm and turned around. A tall, beautiful blonde was smiling up at him. He politely smiled back.

"Hello, my name is Holly."

"Hello Holly. My name is Nicholas."

"This is rather awkward, wouldn't you say?"

"Yes, it's a bit unorthodox to say the least. If it were up to me, I would wine and dine such a beautiful woman as you before I pleasured her."

Nicholas smiled at her quick indrawn breath and the scent of her arousal. *This is going to be a piece of cake*, he thought.

His smiled faltered when he looked up to see the commander staring hard at him. He could swear that he saw regret in her big, beautiful hazel eyes.

He quickly shifted his eyes to the men. He watched as they began to pair off, with one exception...Soren. Soren leaned against a wall watching the scene before him through slanted eyes.

Damn! He hoped he could handle his woman. They all needed to get the job the done.

The blonde was hanging on his arm in a most annoying way, and he wished that she would have chosen someone else. He shook his head. What was wrong with him? This was the exact type of women he normally took to his bed.

Fuck this! He thought as he leaned down and whispered in the blonde's ear. "Let's go back to my quarters. I'm sure that everyone here can take care of themselves while I take care of you."

Holly shivered with anticipation and nodded yes. Nicholas took her hand and began leading her from the room. He turned before they went through the door and saw that the commander was watching their progress. He thought he saw a look of hurt cross her face. What the hell? He had asked her to fuck him. Was he supposed to feel bad that he was now with another woman after her refusal? Well, he didn't, and to prove it he grabbed Holly's sweet little ass and squeezed. But it felt wrong. He was shocked to realize that he would much rather have his hands on the larger ass of the commander.

They hurried to his quarters, and even before he closed the door behind them, Holly pushed him against the door and kissed him. He kissed her back, slipping his tongue in her mouth as she moaned. He once again cupped her ass and she pressed closer to him. She was moaning deep in her throat now, and the scent of her arousal was strong. She unbuttoned his shirt and removed it. Lifting her head from his mouth she moaned, "God, your chest is so hard and sexy." She bent and captured a brown nipple between her teeth.

Nicholas leaned against the wall and watched as her tongue and teeth worked his nipple. It made a very erotic picture and yet he felt nothing. He was almost twelve hundred years old, and for the last hundred years sex had been nothing more than a release. Oh, he received pleasure from the act, but it was more like a bodily function. Insert penis into vagina and pump until you come. It was nothing more than a pleasant feeling to release his semen into a warm vessel. Afterwards, he was relaxed. Most women never even noticed his lack of passion because he made up for it in skill. He could make a woman scream with the most intense orgasm of her life while he planned his next trip in his mind.

His musings stopped when he realized that Holly was undoing his trousers. He pulled her hand away before she could reach in and pull out his flaccid cock. Thinking quickly, he said, "Mmmm baby...let's slow down. I want to pleasure you first."

He pulled her over to the bed and undressed her. He lay back and, tucking her into him with her back to his chest, he played with her nipples while he kissed and sucked on her neck. As she writhed and moaned, he tried to think why he wasn't getting hard for her. He felt no blood rushing in to engorge his cock like it usually did. He felt nothing. *FUCK!* He screamed in his mind. He would have to wear the woman out before she demanded more.

His hand left her nipple and traveled over her flat abdomen to her shaved sex. To make up for his lack of moaning, he began to speak dirty in her ear.

"Oh yeah, baby. Spread those creamy thighs for me. You're so fucking hot."

He rubbed her clit with his thumb as he sank a long finger into her slick opening. She moaned loud. He kept up his assault as he tried to reason why his cock wasn't getting hard.

He'd had a raging hard on yesterday when the commander used him to get off. When he had gotten back to his quarters he'd had to jerk off because he kept picturing the commander's face as she came. He couldn't understand. Maybe it was the drugs they were feeding them. Tomorrow he would ask the others if they were having the same problem. Right now he had to find a way to wear this woman out. He stuck another finger into her and she cried out. His thumb found her swollen clit, and he rubbed it with alternating hard and soft caresses.

"Yesss...Nicholas. That feels so good."

With one hand he fucked her with his fingers, and with his other he moved to her nipple and pulled hard.

She arched off the bed and came in a hot spurt on his hand. His fingers were still inside her when she tried to turn towards him.

"I need you inside me now!"

He did the only thing he could think of. He bit her.

Chapter 6

Holly woke up feeling groggy and disoriented. She remembered having one of the most intense orgasms she'd ever had. Nicholas's fingers had done things to her that were magical. She tried to remember if they'd had sex after that, but her mind was a blank.

She got up to use the bathroom and had her hand on the door handle when she heard a sound from inside. She recognized the sound. It was Nicholas and he was grunting. Holly's breath hitched as she pictured Nicholas in there pulling his cock with his big fist wrapped tightly around it. More than anything she wanted to open the door and watch him as he pleasured himself, but she had a feeling that he would not welcome her company.

She made her way back to the bed and sat down. She was sure now that she and Nicholas did not have sex last night. If they had and he had enjoyed it, he would not be in the bathroom jerking off. He would be inside her.

Holly hung her head. What kind of agent was she? Worse yet, what kind of woman was she? She'd never had trouble getting a man into her bed before. She thought about a certain high ranking UGA officer she had slept with to get this assignment.

She'd easily seduced him. She smiled as she thought about the way she waited at headquarters for everyone to go home. She knew the commander always worked late on a Thursday evening because his wife had her book club that night, and he didn't like to go home to an empty house. She made a pretense of looking for a file on a case she knew he was working on.

"Excuse me Commander, do you have the file on the Brisbane case?"

"Yeah, let me get it for you."

"How many hours have you been working, Commander? You look beat."

"I am beat; I've been here early every morning getting details organized for the Spitsbergen project."

"Awww…let me rub some of the tension out of your shoulders. I worked my way through college as a masseuse."

He had protested, but Holly moved behind his chair and began massaging his shoulders. She leaned in close so her hair would brush the back of his neck. It didn't take long to see the bulge in his pants.

Holly knelt beside his chair "Sir, let me take care of this of this for you. I promise that you'll feel so much better."

He tried removing Holly's hand as it stroked his arousal, but Holly was quick and unzipped his pants and had his cock in her mouth before he could stop her. She sucked him until he was ready to come, and while his head was thrown back she stood and lowered herself onto his cock. His head snapped up, but it was too late. His semen shot into her. Holly almost laughed at the look of devastation on his face. She should be the one who was devastated…she hadn't even gotten off!

Two days later Holly was on a plane headed to Spitsbergen after having a meeting with the commander and telling him that if she wasn't assigned to this project, she was going to tell his wife that they had fucked.

Holly had to be on this project. She was ordered to get on it no matter what she had to do, and now she had failed her mission.

Chapter 7

Jake looked around the room. He was getting admiring glances from some of the women. Jake knew he was appealing, with curly brown hair and light blue eyes. He wasn't the tallest vampire in the room at only 5'10, but he had a body that was hard and muscular.

All of the women were attractive in different ways. His eyes lit up with appreciation when he spotted a large breasted Asian woman who made his mouth water. He started to make a beeline for her when he was intercepted by an attractive, curly haired brunette. Jake smiled at her.

"Howdy. My name is Jake."

"Hi Jake, it's nice to meet you. My name is Nette. Are you by any chance a cowboy?"

Jake smiled at the woman. Like a lot of women this one must have a fantasy about riding a cowboy. Well, Jake had taken quite a few ladies for a ride in his long life.

"I used to be a cowboy, back in the day of cattle rustling and wagon trains. These days most would call me a rancher. I still ride a horse, but I also drive a Chevy truck."

The woman was practically drooling on Jake's feet. This was going to be easier than he thought. He wouldn't have to seduce this one or play any games. He bet that he'd be inside her within the hour.

The woman put her hand on his arm and leaned close to whisper in his ear. "I have to admit that I've always had fantasies about big strapping cowboys."

"Is that so, darlin'? Well, just you wait until you see just how big ole Jake is."

Nette giggled and ran her hand up his arm. "Why don't we go back to your place and see what happens?"

Nette's eyes sparkled with mischief, and Jake was mesmerized.

"Um, sure. I don't think we need to stick around here."

Jake was hard. Harder than he'd ever been in his life. He was having a hard time walking with his stiff, aching cock pushing against his jeans. As soon as they hit his room he was going to toss her on his bed and fuck the ever-living daylights out of her.

When they got to his door, Jake turned to take Nette in his arms, but she sidestepped him.

"Whoa big fella, let's get inside first."

Jake quickly opened the door and pulled Nette inside. As soon as he had the door closed he grabbed her and slanted his mouth over hers. Nette wrapped her arms around him and kissed him back.

Holy crap, could this woman kiss. She swept her tongue in his mouth and softly stroked his until he heard himself moaning. At the same time she reached down and began stroking his cock through his jeans. Moving her mouth, she found a sensitive spot behind his right ear that she began to nip with her teeth. He wasn't sure what the hell her hand was doing to his cock, but it felt damn good. When she increased the friction he bellowed.

"FUCK!"

Without any warning he came hot and hard inside his jeans. He was breathing hard.

"What the fuck was that? I've never come from having my cock rubbed for ten seconds before."

Nette smiled sweetly at him.

"I'm sorry. You were so worked up, and I thought you could use a little release."

"Damn, woman. I wanted to release inside of you. Not in my pants as if I'm a greenhorn."

Again she smiled sweetly.

"Don't worry Jake. You can still come inside me."

Jake looked at her as if she was crazy.

"Well, I hate to burst your bubble Nette, but it will take a while before I'll be able to do that again."

Again with that sweet smile and twinkle in her eye. It was beginning to make Jake leery.

Nette stood before him and opened his jeans, and pulling them down, knelt in front of him. Jake closed his eyes, waiting for her hot little mouth to start sucking his cock. His eyes flew open when she grabbed his sac and began rolling his balls between her hands.

"Sweet mercy!" Jake groaned. He felt his cock spring to life.

On her knees in front of him, Nette gasped when she saw how thick he was.

"Oh my. Your cock is wide."

He smiled with pleasure. Now that was how things usually went when he fucked a woman. They all were astounded at his width.

She stood and went to pick up a small overnight bag that he hadn't seen her carry in.

"What's in the bag?"

"Some things that will help us have a little fun."

"Um...what kind of things?" Jake asked suspiciously.

Nette reached in the bag and pulled out a pair of leather chaps.

Jake groaned. This woman was loco. All he wanted to do was fuck her senseless and bind her to him so that she would be willing to help them. He had seen Nicholas leave with the tall, stunning blonde woman earlier. He was probably getting the ride of his life, while he was stuck here with a ball grabbing, cock rubbing, chap wearing loon. When he saw her bring out a holster and two cans of whipped cream, he headed for the door.

Nette cut him off.

"Jake, please wear the chaps for me! I promise that you won't be disappointed."

Jake kept the picture of his ranch in his mind as he went into the bathroom and stripped naked. All he had to do was put up with this crazy woman for a few days and he'd be free to go back to fucking normal women.

His ranch, and the people who worked there, were his family. They lived a quiet, peaceful life. Things were orderly. Jake liked order in his life. Just because he had been turned vampire didn't mean his life had to be full of chaos.

He felt like a dang blasted fool walking out of the bathroom in nothing but a leather pair of chaps, with his now limp dick and his ass hanging out. He stopped dead in his tracks when he spotted Nette, wearing nothing but the holster with the two cans of whipped cream, standing with one leg raised on a chair.

She was magnificent. Her breasts were perfect round porcelain globes with rosy pink nipples. Her sex was partially shaved and plump. He could see the pink folds glistening with her desire. And God, her legs were long and shapely. He felt his shaft harden, and Nette slowly and seductively sauntered over to him.

"Why cowboy, you look positively delicious."

She knelt in front of him and took the broad head of his cock into her mouth. He wrapped his hands in her hair. Like their kiss before, her tongue was like soft silk wrapping around his shaft. In all his years he had never felt anything so damn good. She sucked and licked and nipped until he couldn't bear it anymore. His legs started shaking. He pulled her head back by her hair.

"Nette, I'm not playing anymore. I need to fuck you right now."

He picked her up and tossed her on the bed. He crawled on top of her, but in one swift movement she rolled them over and, grabbing his cock, sank down on it.

"My God Nette...don't stop. Ride me baby. You're so hot."

Nette rode his thick cock in a slow steady pace. Jake felt like he would go mad from the feeling of her tight muscles pulling on his cock.

Nette leaned forward, and un-holstering the cans of whipped cream used them to cover each nipple.

She lowered her mouth and sucked hard.

With each pull and tug of a nipple Jake felt his balls tighten. He began to buck his hips hard. He knew he didn't have much longer so he rolled them over and pounded into her with a power he'd never felt before.

Nette screamed, "God Jake...don't stop."

He felt the climax begin for her as her muscles clenched all around him like a vice. He lifted her legs in the air and slammed into her with everything he had. He came with a triumphant cry that mingled with hers.

Jake lay there in disbelief. His head was spinning. This woman who he'd just met, this crazy, insane woman, had rocked his world upside down.

Chapter 8

Nette attempted to turn over and couldn't help the groan that escaped her. She was already sore from using muscles that she hadn't used in a long time.

"Are you okay darlin'?" Jake asked beside her.

"Yeah, I'm fine, just a little sore from your crazy sexcapades."

Jake laughed and Nette's heart jumped. No one, not man or vampire, should have such a rich, heartfelt laugh like that.

"Here, let me help you with that," Jake said, rubbing her shoulders.

Nette felt herself relax under Jake's strong hands. The man was a marvel. He was more reserved than the men she had previously been involved with. Not that there were that many of them. Oh, she knew that most people thought she was a wild one, and she would be the first to admit that she'd had her moments over the years, but all in all, she could count her lovers on one hand.

Nette was born with a natural zest for life. Everything held a fascination for her, from the stars in the sky to a single blade of grass. People who got to know her well were always amazed that she had such a positive outlook on life, especially when she told them that she had grown up in foster homes. She was told that she was left in a hospital in Baltimore. The way she looked at it; her mother had cared enough about her to make sure that she would be safe; otherwise she would have thrown her into a dumpster somewhere.

Jake's hands were amazing as they moved from her shoulders to her back. He used just the right amount of pressure as he took long stokes down her back.

"Oh my God…you are good," she moaned.

Jake leaned down close to her ear and whispered, "That's exactly what you said to me when I was sliding in and out of your sweet body."

Nette's whole body shuddered. "Ummm cowboy…you're making me ache in an all together different way now."

Jake began kissing her back, his soft lips trailing down her spine.

"So, what's with your fascination with cowboys anyway?"

"When I was thirteen I was sent to a new foster family and my foster dad, Walter, loved the old cowboy movies. On weekends I would stay up and we watched old Gene Autry movies until the wee hours of the morning. I was sad when he and his wife were killed in a car accident. I only got to stay with them nine months."

Jake's lips had stilled. He asked her, "How many foster families were you with?"

"Eight of them, I think. When I turned eighteen the last family threw me out because they didn't receive any money anymore."

"Threw you out? What the hell kind of people were they?"

Nette shrugged. "Life was hard for them. I didn't hold any grudges."

Jake rolled her over and his eyes were dark and intense.

"How is it that you can forgive so easily?"

"Why wouldn't I, Jake? Who wants to go through life with their insides all tangled up with anger? I'd much rather be tangled up with laughter and love. Besides, everything happens for a reason. After they threw me out I lived for awhile in a shelter, and I met a volunteer there who worked for UGA. They took me in, sent me to college, and gave me a job afterwards."

Jake ran a hand through his hair. "Why did you volunteer for this assignment, Nette? What made you come here willing to have sex with a stranger?"

Nette took his hand. "Because you needed me to."

Jake kissed her then. The kiss was soft and sweet, and Nette felt her heart melting. This vampire was nothing like she thought he'd be. Sure, she had expected the wild sex, but she had never expected him to touch her heart.

Chapter 9

Tor eyed the women that remained. Two of his brother vampires had already left with their women. He had his eye on the tall, dark haired woman, but she seemed too polished to pick the likes of him. Tor didn't kid himself…he intimidated most women. At almost seven feet tall, his size alone would discourage most of the women in the room. Add to that the long blond hair, a nose that was a little bit crooked from being broken before he turned vampire, and the fact that he tended to dress like a biker, it was easy to understand their reluctance. The funny thing was that of all the vampires in the room, he was the least likely to be violent.

As he stood there waiting for a woman to pick him, he checked each one out, admiring their assets. The woman with the big breasts was headed over, and beside him Blayze said, "This must be my lucky day."

The women stopped directly in front of Tor.

"Hello. I'm Juls."

Tor, misunderstanding the situation, said, "Hello, my name is Tor, and this is Blayze. Excuse me."

He turned to go and a small hand on his arm stopped him.

"I think you misunderstood me, Tor. I came over to talk with you."

At this Blayze laughed and said, "Excuse me," and walked away.

Tor looked down at the tiny woman, way down. She barely reached his chest.

"Ah, look Juls…you can't be serious."

"Why not?"

Tor looked around and bent far down to say in a quiet voice, "Well, you're a tiny little thing, and I'm so large."

Jules looked up at him with a puzzled expression.

Bending down again he said, "*I'm large.*"

Juls continued to stare at him.

Oh for God's sake, Tor thought. Does this woman need for me to draw a picture? He bent down once more.

"I've got a very large penis."

"So?"

Tor raked a hand though his long blond hair.

"You're very small."

Again she said, "So?"

Tor, who never got frustrated, felt his nerves getting rattled.

"I don't think I'll fit."

"Why?"

Tor wanted to be done with this conversation, and in a voice that was louder than he thought he yelled, "MY PENIS IS TOO LARGE!"

The entire room got quiet, and then a woman said in a serious, questioning voice, "Um, is there such a thing as a too large penis?"

The room exploded in laughter, and Tor had enough.

He grabbed the girl's hand and pulled her from the room, but not before hearing, "Seriously. Can a penis be too large?"

Tor didn't know where else to head but his quarters. Once there he intended to explain to this tiny woman about male anatomy. Maybe he would have to draw her a picture.

Hopefully, when they got back, one of the other women would still want him. The whole thing was humiliating. He knew Nicholas's plan was a good one, but he felt like a piece of meat in that room.

Tor pushed the girl into the room ahead of him and turned to close the door. When he turned around she was right before him and reached up high, pulled his head down, and put her lips on his.

Her kiss was soft and sweet, and before he knew it he was kissing her back with urgency. His cock began to ache and that brought him to his senses. He pulled back and extracted himself from her embrace.

"Juls, we can't do this. You are hot, but it's not physically possible. I might hurt you, and I don't want to do that."

She eyed the large bulge in his pants.

"Can't we at least try?"

He shook his head. "No, I might not be able to stop and hurt you by accident."

"Please?"

Tor ran a hand over his face. What the fuck? He had a gorgeous woman begging him to fuck her and he couldn't. Why were the fates so cruel?

"No."

"Yes."

"Juls...."

"Tor...."

He took a stand and crossed his arms over his chest.

"No!" He repeated.

Tor took a step back at the anger in Juls's eyes. Then he took another step back when she got a sly smile on her face. He wondered what the hell she was up to.

Juls began undoing the buttons on her red silk blouse.

"Stop that!" Tor shouted at her.

She just smiled a sexy as hell smile and continued.

"I mean it Juls. This can't happen."

When all the buttons were undone Juls suggestively pulled the blouse off one shoulder.

Tor put a hand over his mouth so she wouldn't hear his groan. She was wearing a fucking red lace bra that barely kept her large breasts in place. The creamy swell was spilling over.

Juls continued and slipped the other shoulder out and let the red silk slide down her body. Tor was transfixed. He wanted so badly to turn his back on her but couldn't.

She continued her striptease by wiggling her hips to slide her skirt down her body until it pooled at her high heeled feet. Tor stared at the red thong that barely concealed her glistening sex. He had no idea that he was rubbing his hard and aching erection as he watched her.

"Holy shit, Juls. Don't do it."

Tor moaned as Juls reached behind her and unclasped her bra and let it fall to the floor. Her breasts were glorious; firm, round, and large with two dark nipples that were standing erect. Tor felt his legs shaking. He was holding on by a thread.

The thread broke when Juls slid her hands under her breasts and lifted them in offering to the blond warrior.

Tor let out a muffled curse and slowly began to walk towards her. Two can play at her game, he thought.

He circled her, not touching her. He stopped behind her, leaned down, and let his breath touch the back of her neck. He smiled when he saw her shiver. Before backing away he let his lips brush her neck lightly. It was her turn to moan.

Standing close in front of her, he reached down and lifted his black t-shirt over his head, exposing a broad, smooth chest with well defined abs. Bending, he took off his boots. He never looked away from her as he opened his jeans. He lowered them inch-by-inch, reveling at the heat in her eyes. He moaned when his aching cock sprang free. He saw Juls's eyes widen at his size.

He kicked off his jeans and wrapped his fist around his throbbing cock. He watched Juls as he slid his fist up and down the long length. His breathing becoming rapid, and he began to pump faster. He moaned while he watched Juls's hand dip into her red panties, and his hand pumped harder.

Juls was moaning and sliding her fingers in and out of her slick opening. Tor knew he was going to come any minute, and he didn't want to waste it on his hand.

With a curse he swept Juls up in his arms and tossed her on the bed. She opened her thighs to receive him but he shook his head no, and instead crawled up her body until his cock lay between her large breasts.

Knowing his intensions, Juls held her breasts together and cried out as he began to pump his hips.

"Fuck Juls...you're so hot. Your tits drive me wild."

He pumped his cock between her tits faster and faster. He thought he would lose his mind from the pleasure.

Juls let go of her breasts and grabbed Tor's head.

"Tor, please. Please at least try. I need you. I've never wanted anyone as much as I want you."

Those words were Tor's undoing. He slid down and spread her legs apart. Kneeling between her legs he spread her open. She was wet and ready. He closed his eyes and prayed for patience. He took his cock in his hand and put the head at her entrance, and watched transfixed as it disappeared inside her. He forced himself to stay still as he prepared to slide another inch forward. Sweat broke out on his forehead as he fought for control. It didn't help that Juls was moaning and writhing on the bed, or that her juices were getting his fingers all wet and slick.

"Lay still woman!" he choked out.

"Ohhh Tor...fuck me. I need you inside me so bad it aches. Please Tor. I'm begging you."

God help us, he thought as he plunged in her. Once he started he couldn't stop. She was so tight and wet. He kept asking her, "Are you all right?"

"Yessss...," she moaned. "Don't stop."

"Baby, I couldn't stop if I tried. I want to fuck you until you come hard. I want to give you an orgasm that rocks your luscious little body, and then I'm going to start all over again. I'm going to lick you until you come hot in my mouth, and while you're still coming I'm gonna slam my cock into you fast and hard."

Juls screamed as she found her release. Tor tried to hold off, but when he felt her muscles tightening around his cock he threw his head back and roared as he spurted hotly inside her.

Tor rolled over so she was on top. He brushed the hair out of her face.

"Hey…are you okay?"

She smiled at him. "I'm better than okay."

He pulled her down beside of him and tucked her by his side because she sounded sleepy.

"Tor?"

"Yeah?"

"You fit perfectly."

"I know."

"You were wrong."

"I was wrong."

"Tor?"

He sighed. "Yeah?"

"There is no such thing as too big."

Chapter 11

Juls ran her tongue up the long, long length of Tor's cock. She just wanted one more taste. She had only slept an hour before she wanted more of this vampire.

Tor pulled her up to tuck her against his side. "God woman. Don't you ever get enough? That was without a doubt the best blow job I've ever had."

Juls smiled. Little did he know that it was the first time she had ever tasted a man. She wasn't going to tell him that though. He didn't need to know about her lack of experience.

"You were right about being too large for me...at least for my mouth." Juls chuckled.

Tor turned over to face her. "I don't think so. As a matter of fact, I think your hot little mouth is perfect. Can I ask you something, Juls?"

"Sure."

"Why did you pick me out of all the vampires in that room? I would have thought that you would have gone for someone more like Blayze."

Juls looked at his handsome face. He was clearly puzzled. She felt like she owed him the truth.

"You were the only one who looked dangerous. You wear your hair long, and I bet that at one point your nose was broken in a fight. Your biker boots aren't just for show. They're worn and well used. Plus, you're huge. All together, this stuff spells bad boy."

Tor seemed a little disappointed when he said, "Ah, I get it. You get turned on by the bad boys."

Juls sighed. "You don't understand at all, do you?"

"No, I don't think I do."

Juls didn't want to tell him of her shameful past. But he probably deserved to understand why she chose him.

"A little over a year ago I was living in a small country that is part of Malaysia. My life was one of wealth and comfort. I now know how spoiled and overindulged I was. My family was one of importance, and when I turned twenty-five, I was to marry a man I'd never met in an arrangement made between my family and one from a neighboring country. My husband-to-be arrived a week before the wedding, and when I met him I was so relieved to find that he was handsome and had impeccable manners."

What Juls wouldn't tell him was that her family wasn't just another important family, but rulers of that tiny country. That was something she would never tell anyone. Juls remembered how enamored she was of the handsome man. How everyone in her family was bowled over by his charm. Somehow he had fooled them all.

"Two days before the wedding he knocked on my bedroom door. When I opened it he pushed me inside and said vile, ugly things to me."

Juls felt Tor stiffen beside her, but she was determined to get the whole sorry story out. This was the first time she'd talked about it since that night.

"He told me that I was a tease and a whore and that I should be grateful he wanted to fuck me at all. He threw me on the bed and covered my mouth with his hand, then yelled for me to open my legs, and when I refused he slapped me. So I opened my legs. He tore off my panties and opened his pants. Then he pushed inside me, and it felt like I was being torn in two. Thankfully it didn't last too long. Before he left he said that I was a cold fish, and next time I'd better please him or he would beat me."

Juls was grateful that Tor had kept quiet. This was hard enough to get out. She was also grateful for the soothing touch of his hand that kept smoothing her hair back.

"I went to my father and told him what had happened. You can imagine my surprise when my father slapped me too and told me in no uncertain terms what he would do to me if I ruined this alliance. So I went back to my room, packed a bag, and left. I looked up a friend from boarding school and went to stay with her until I could figure out what to do. It turned out my friend's father was a commander with UGA and offered me a job, and here I am."

Juls waited for Tor to say something. She was afraid that he wouldn't understand.

"And here you are. Volunteering for an assignment that would require you to have sex, and I'm guessing it's the first sex you've had since that horrific night. And who do you pick to have sex with? Not any of the men who are polished and well mannered. No, you go for the exact opposite of the bastard that raped you."

Juls couldn't stop the tears that fell as Tor cupped her face gently in his hands.

"You are a brave and amazing woman, Juls. My God, when I think how passionate and loving you are after what has happened to you, it humbles me to know that you picked me to trust."

Tor wiped the tears from her face, and she was glad that she had picked him. Somehow she knew that she could trust him. He confirmed that when he said, "Don't worry, Princess, your secret will always be safe with me."

She couldn't help smiling.

Chapter 12

Garrett watched as the blonde woman approached from his left. Out of all of the women this was the one he was hoping would approach him. She was tall and blonde and had a fantastic body. Even though she wore a modest pair of black pants and white sweater, Garrett could tell her body was well toned. Fitness was important to him. His blond hair and tan, not to mention his six-pack of abs, was constantly getting him picked on by the other guys. All of the vampires had taking to calling him "Dude." Before becoming vampire he had been an avid surfer and was a professional trainer.

Out of all of the vampires here, he was the youngest, just having been made vampire fifteen years ago. He was still trying to get used to everything.

Standing before him, the blonde smiled.

"Hi, my name is Tamika. How are you?"

Garrett laughed. "Hi, Tamika. My name is Garrett."

Still smiling she asked, "Why are you laughing at me?"

"It just struck me funny that you ask how I am all polite like, while we're smack in the middle of some crazy shit."

Tamika laughed as well. "I guess you have a point. All of this is a bit unorthodox."

He liked her smile. She reminded him of the girls from the beach who ran or played volleyball back when he was human. Her Australian accent was sexy as hell.

His smile faded as he thought about what he had to do. He couldn't get sidetracked from his assignment.

"Uh…listen, I know that this is way messed up and really kind of creepy, but do you want to do this with me?"

Tamika cocked her head to the side and appeared to be taking his measure.

"Yeah, I do."

Garrett took her hand and led her from the room. As they walked back to his quarters he was excited and really happy that if he had to do such a bizarre thing, at least it was with a woman like Tamika.

Garrett opened the door and let Tamika enter first. He flipped a switch to turn on the lights and Tamika stared at the sparse room.

"Yeah. They don't give us too much."

Tamika mumbled, "Sorry."

"Well, it's not like it's your fault, and you are here trying to help us."

Now that they were alone, Tamika looked nervous.

Shit, thought Garrett. I'm blowing this.

He needed to come through for the others.

He noticed Tamika looking at the weights on the floor in the corner of the room.

"I stole those from our exercise area. I have a habit of doing twenty reps before going to sleep. You aren't going to tell on me, are you?" He asked playfully.

"No. Your secret is safe with me. I have my own habits. I always take a five mile run before breakfast. If for some reason I can't, I get cranky."

"Why don't we sit?"

Garrett led Tamika over to the bed and pulled her down beside him. Seeing her hands shaking, he sat with his hands gripping the sides of the bed. He had to admit that despite their obvious common interests, he wasn't feeling her. Great…this is just great, he thought. He had to at least try.

"Would it be okay if I kissed you?"

"I suppose so."

Garrett tilted her chin up with his fingers and lowered his mouth to hers. He kissed her gently and opened his mouth slightly to trace her lips with his tongue. Her lips were pursed tightly, and he felt like he was kissing a statue.

He pulled his head back and asked, "Anything?"

She shook her head. "I'm sorry. I guess we just don't have any chemistry."

Garrett sighed. "I guess you're right. Would you like me to walk you back to the common room?"

"Is it all right if I stay here for a little while? Just the thought of going back there is giving me a headache."

"Sure. No problem," was what he said, but all he was thinking was he needed to get back and find a woman to fuck or Nicholas was going to chew his ass out.

"Is it all right if I just lay my head down here for a little while? I really do have a headache."

"Sure, go right ahead. I'll just, um…go to the bathroom."

Garrett went into the small bathroom. Christ! This was a total fucking disaster. He was a crap vampire. Vampires were supposed to make women swoon. They were hot, sexy creatures that fucked their way through anything. He couldn't believe he was hiding in the goddamn bathroom.

He opened the door, ready to tell the woman to get off his bed and out of his room, and saw that she was sleeping.

"Shit."

Garrett didn't have the heart to wake her up. Not knowing what else to do, he thought he might as well do some reps. He grabbed a pair of shorts and went back in the bathroom to change.

He came out wearing only the shorts. He picked up his weights and began doing his nightly reps. He knew it was a foolish thing to do since exercise had no effect on a vampire, but it let him feel almost normal while he did it.

Garrett got lost in the motion of slowly bringing the fifty pound weight up to his chest and lowering it to his waist. He watched as the veins on his bicep popped. A fine sheen of sweat developed on his body and still he continued.

His back was turned to the bed, so he never saw Tamika get up and walk to stand behind him. He felt a warm hand on his bare back and he made to turn around.

"No. Don't turn around." Tamika's voice was husky, and for the first time since bringing her back to his room he felt the stir of blood to his groin.

"Keep doing the reps. I find it very sexy."

Garrett continued with the reps as her hands roamed over his back.

"I love how your muscles bunch and stretch. I bet you're strong."

Garrett felt his cock getting hard under his thin shorts. It was hot having her hands lightly running over him without his seeing her.

He jerked when her hands grabbed his ass.

"Oh, I love how hard and tight your ass is."

Okay, Garrett couldn't think straight now. Looking down, he saw his erection had pitched a tent in his shorts.

She let her hands slide into the waistband of his shorts and began kneading his bare buttocks. She was breathing hard and clearly excited, which turned Garrett on even more. Her hands moved towards the front of his body and he felt her fingertips brush lightly through his pubic hair. She was being careful not to touch his straining erection, and it was driving him wild.

"God Tamika, you're making me so hot," he rasped. He was having a hard time keeping a hold on the weights that he had let drop to his side.

When Tamika tentatively swept her fingers over his cock, he dropped the weights and put his hands on the wall in front of him.

"Stay there."

Garrett felt her step away and heard her peeling off her clothes. When she returned she pressed her naked body against his back. Garrett sucked in a deep breath as she rubbed her breasts against his bare back. She pulled on his shorts, tugging them down around his ankles, and he stepped out of them.

Tamika reached an arm around his waist and grasped his cock in her hand.

"Yessss...squeeze it tight, baby."

When she applied more pressure he growled low in his throat and started to pump his hips.

She slid her other hand down his ass and between his legs and cupped his sac.

"Fuck, that feels sooo good."

Tamika applied pressure and Garrett went crazy. He swung around, grabbed her, and threw her against the wall. In one swift motion he lifted her leg and guided his cock inside her.

Tamika groaned, and that was all the encouragement he needed. He pounded into her over and over again.

"Oh my God, I'm going to come, Garrett."

"Go ahead baby, come. I've got you."

Tamika cried out and Garrett felt her muscles pulling at his cock. He lifted her up and she wrapped her legs around his waist. Holding her close, he brushed her long blonde hair while murmuring in her ear.

"I've got you baby...come for me...that's it...God, you feel so good."

She finally lifted her head.

"You didn't come. I'm sorry."

Garrett smiled and kissed her. "We're not done yet."

Garrett started walking towards the bed with his cock still deep inside her, and the motion caused a most delicious friction that made him groan with each step.

Tamika took advantage of the situation and began to clench her vaginal muscles.

"Fuck meeee! What the hell are you doing to me?" Garrett groaned.

Tamika let out a small sexy laugh, and Garrett felt it down to his balls.

"It's a little exercise I do everyday. I have great control over every muscle in my body." To prove her point, she clenched her muscles tightly around his cock.

Garrett tried to hold back, but her muscles were milking him. He threw his head back and with a roar felt his hot seed come rushing forth.

When the last shudder swept threw him, he walked over to the bed, and with her still connected to his body, lay down.

"I don't have the words to describe how awesome that was."

Tamika kissed his mouth. "That is just the beginning. I told you I have great control over every muscle in my body. Did you know that the tongue is also a muscle?"

Garrett felt his cock stir.

Chapter 13

"Can I use your weights?" Tamika asked Garrett. Even after two bouts of hot sex she needed some controlled physical release. Exercise had become as necessary to her as breathing.

"Sure. Let me help you," Garrett said as he got up and, pulling on those sexy shorts, went over to the weights. "What do you normally lift?" he asked, looking over his shoulder at her.

Tamika rose and, spotting one of Garrett's t-shirts, slipped it over her head. She smiled when Garrett said, "Damn, you look good in my shirt."

Tamika knelt beside him. "I've never lifted weights before."

"In that case we better start easy. How about twenty-five pounds?"

"Sounds good."

They stood and Garrett stepped behind her and guided her through a few reps. He sat on a chair and watched her.

"You're so beautiful," he said softly.

Tamika let the weights fall to her sides.

"Don't say that. I hate hearing people call me beautiful."

"You're kidding, right? Most women love being called beautiful. Damn, I like being called beautiful." Garrett laughed. He stopped laughing when he saw Tamika's eyes fill with tears.

"Hey, I'm sorry. I really thought you were joking."

Tamika set the weights on the floor and sat down in the chair opposite him. She took a deep breath. She hated telling this story. Even after six years she was still ashamed. Taking a deep breath she began.

"When I was sixteen, I was working as a waitress in a restaurant in Sydney. During a shift one day, I was approached by a guy who asked if I ever did any modeling."

Garrett snorted, "Sounds like a pick up line to me."

Tamika nodded her agreement. "That's what I thought at first, but he gave me a card with a well known agency name on it. When I showed it to my mom, she insisted that I give it a shot."

She remembered how excited her mom had been. She was sure that it was their ticket to better days.

"The very next day we went to the agency and I was signed. Right away I began getting jobs. Mostly small ad campaigns, but it was getting me noticed. A year later I was being considered for a major ad campaign with commercials and billboards. The agency flew my mom and me to Los Angeles for interviews."

Tamika remembered how excited her Mom was. "'Just think, baby girl, this job could lead to bigger things for us. You may get offered parts in movies. Maybe I can get a small part in one of them. I'm still in pretty good shape. You know that in high school I was the star in the spring play. Everyone said I had talent and that I could make something out of myself. If only I hadn't let myself be taken advantage of by your father!'"

Tamika had heard this story her whole life. Her mom blamed everyone but herself for her failures. She had ended up alone and bitter and would always be so.

"Go on."

Tamika came back to the present day with Garrett's softly spoken words. She looked at him and could tell by the hardening of his face that he knew this was not going to be a happily ever after story. He was right.

"There were a lot of girls at the audition, all young and beautiful. The head of casting, James Engelwood, was a middle-aged man that looked at the girls like he would devour them. I could sense the wrongness that was inside him."

Tamika shivered but kept going, "After my audition I saw my mom talking to Mr. Engelwood. Afterwards she was excited and told me that I had made the final cut and would have a second audition that night. The second audition, I found out, was in Mr. Engelwood's hotel room."

"Son of a bitch," Garrett hissed.

"When I realized what was happening I turned to leave, and my mom slapped me so hard she split my lip. She screamed that I wasn't going to ruin her life again. It was then that I saw the bitterness had eaten away at her soul, and she would never stop blaming me for the way her life turned out. I pushed her out of the way and ran.

"The first year was the hardest. I lived on the streets mostly. I got a job waitressing and eventually saved up enough to get a room. I lucked out and got a job in an upscale restaurant, and was able to earn enough to take some classes at the community college. It was there that I met a professor with ties to the UGA, and here I am."

Tamika looked up and was surprised to see Garrett kneeling on the floor beside her chair.

"You survived a year living on the streets of Los Angeles. That's why you train and exercise everyday. You need to be stronger than them." His eyes were filled with admiration.

She stared into his kind face. He may be vampire but he had shown her more compassion and love than many humans had shown her throughout her life. And his strength made her feel stronger.

Chapter 14

Eduardo looked over the women in the room. All of them were attractive in some way. It would not be a hardship to have sex with any one of them. In his long vampire life he had never met a woman he wouldn't want to fuck. He took large women, old women, beautiful women, and ugly women to his bed. His looks guaranteed him that all women were attracted to him. He was, after all, Latino. He wore his coal black hair on the long side, just reaching his collar. Just one look from his smoldering dark eyes could make women come. Women would go on for hours about his soft full lips and a mouth they swore was magic.

Across the room he watched as a woman rose from her chair. Every male eye watched as she sashayed across the room. Eduardo admired her wicked curves. She was wearing a tight black dress that accentuated large breasts and an ass that J Lo would envy.

Eduardo smiled as she stopped in front of him. He knew that this beautiful creature would pick him.

"Hello, my name is Samantha. Has anyone ever told you that you look like Antonio Banderas?" She extended her hand to shake, but Eduardo brought it to his mouth and kissed her hand softly.

"Samantha, it's my pleasure to meet you. And since I am older by a few hundred years, Antonio Banderas looks like me."

She laughed, and the soft sound stirred his cock to life.

"This is a most unusual way to meet, no?"

"Yes it is, but then again so is a singles bar."

Eduardo laughed. "That is true, *mi querida*. But as long as the end result is pleasurable, what does it matter?"

"Well? Would you like to see if we're compatible?"

Eduardo liked her boldness. "Si, let's go to my quarters. But I'm sure there will be no question of us being compatible."

Eduardo led the beauty to his quarters. Opening the door, he allowed her to enter before him. He smiled, quite proud of the fact that though he was a vampire, he was still a gentleman. Once inside, Eduardo closed the door and moved to stand close to Samantha.

"You are in for a treat, Senorita Samantha. I've had many years to practice the art of lovemaking."

"Well, that's good to know, but I require other types of stimulation first."

Eduardo smiled. "Ah...you would like to kiss me?"

Whatever the woman was thinking about clearly excited her as her breathing became rapid, and the scent of her arousal hung heavy in the air. When her pink little tongue darted out to lick her lips, Eduardo smiled. He knew exactly what she wanted, and he was more than willing to let her have her way.

"Ahhhh...I know what you want *querida*, and I am more than happy to let you have your way."

She smiled a very sexy smile and, reaching behind her, began to unzip her dress. He watched with hooded eyes as she slid out of the sleeves and let the dress drop to pool at her feet. Eduardo sucked in a breath; she wore nothing under the dress. Her full breasts were perfect globes of creamy flesh topped with large pink nipples that hardened under his gaze. Her hips flared wide, giving her the luscious curves that he and all the other vampires admired earlier. Her sex was shaved, which he preferred. It allowed him a better view of his magnificent cock when a woman rode him.

Samantha slowly walked towards him. "You are still in your clothes? Would you like me to help you take them off?"

"Of course, *querida*. That's what I was waiting for."

For some reason she chuckled, then stripped him of his jacket and began to unbutton his shirt. She kissed each inch of flesh that she exposed.

"Your chest is so hard. Are all your other parts as hard as this?'

He growled low in his throat. "You will soon find out."

She finished with his shirt and let it drop to the floor. She kissed his neck while she opened his black trousers. Trailing kisses down his chest, she sank to her knees as she pulled his trousers all the way down.

She sucked in a breath as she stared at the long, thick cock jutting out in front of her. She had the glint of appreciation in her eyes that he had seen so often in the eyes of the women he fucked.

"You are magnificent."

"Thank you, *querida*. Would you like to do this here, or should we move to the bed?"

"Oh, I think it will be more comfortable on the bed, don't you?"

"Of course," he said, though he would have preferred her on her knees in front of him while she sucked him off. Oh well, he would do what he needed to. Nicholas and the others were counting on him. He kicked his trousers away and followed her to the bed, admiring her ass as he went.

They climbed into the narrow bed and lay side by side on their backs. Eduardo folded his arms under his head in his usual relaxed position, waiting for the woman to pleasure him.

Okay…what the hell was taking her so long? He turned his head to look over at her. She was lying just as he was, with her arms under her head, her eyes closed and her legs bent and parted.

OH HELL NO! He sat up. In all his long years he had never done that to a woman, nor had a woman ever expected him to. Women always pleasured him…that was how it worked.

Samantha sat up. "Is something wrong?"

"Um…no. Everything is fine. I just have a…a slight cramp in my leg. I'll be right back. I need to walk and stretch it."

"Okay, but hurry up. I can't wait to feel your tongue inside me."

He didn't even acknowledge her as he raced to the bathroom.

"*Hija de puta!*" He swore as soon as he closed the door. What was he going to do? He had never gone down on a woman before. He didn't even know what to do. Sex for him had always been all about the women pleasuring him. He would lie back and let them work their magic on him, and then they would mount him and ride him until he would come. The women were always happy afterwards. No one had ever complained.

Eduardo rubbed a hand over his face. He knew he had to do this. He had to somehow give this woman pleasure or Nicholas's plan wouldn't work. He couldn't be the only vampire that couldn't get the job done.

Squaring his shoulders, he looked down at his now limp cock hanging between his legs.

"*Mierda.*"

With a sigh he opened the door and walked slowly to the bed.

Samantha purred. "I'm glad you're back. I was going to start without you."

"Why didn't you?" He mumbled.

"What?"

"Nothing. Why don't you lie back and get ready for me?"

Eduardo closed his eyes and counted to three. He'd faced countless enemies over the years, and he'd never known what fear was until now.

Opening his eyes, he looked at the place where he was supposed to use his tongue to pleasure the woman. He had never seen it like this before and he found himself curious. It was smooth and pale, with little pink folds peeking out. As he sat there watching, Samantha squirmed on the bed.

"The way you're staring at me is hot," she said breathlessly.

Maybe he could just sit there and stare at her until she got off.

"Touch me."

Well, he was wrong about that one. Kneeling between her creamy thighs, he ran a hand up the inside of her leg and let it lightly graze her slit. He raised an eyebrow when she hissed.

So far so good. His attention was caught by the pink folds that he saw were now glistening. He cautiously touched a finger to a pink fold.

"It's wet," he marveled.

"Oh God, yeah. I'm wet for you."

Feeling pleased that he was at least doing something right, he wanted to see more. Bringing his other hand down, he pinched either side of her slit and spread her open wide. He was fascinated. He could see the hole where his cock would enter.

It looked too small. He looked down at his cock, which had somehow come back to life. He doubted that he would fit in this woman's hole.

"Touch me, please," she begged.

He came out of his daze, and using a finger he traced a circle around the hole.

Samantha thrashed her head on the pillow.

"Did you like that?" He asked, curious.

"Fuck yeah. You're so good. Your teasing is driving me fucking crazy."

He was pleased with himself. He could do this. He could please the woman. Holding her open again, this time with one hand, he took his finger and swirled it around her hole. This time she was very wet and slippery, and as his finger swirled it slipped partially into her hole.

Samantha's back arched off the bed.

"God...don't stop. More."

Eduardo was finding this quite enjoyable, and he plunged his finger into her slick opening. He began a slow rhythm of in and out. The fingers on his other hand began an exploration. When his index finger scraped over a little nub, Samantha bucked her hips hard.

"That feels sooo good," she moaned.

Eduardo was a quick learner, and soon he was teasing the little nub until, to his surprise, it began to swell and throb. Samantha's head was thrashing back and forth, and he was getting turned on by her low moans. He hoped that she would soon say that he should stop and mount him.

"For fuck's sake, taste me…taste me now."

Uh oh. She still wanted him to put his mouth on her. She would know that he hadn't done that before and he wouldn't be able to please her.

"Please…," she begged.

With a small sigh he removed his finger from her warmth and repositioned himself between her legs. He had to go in.

Eduardo dipped his head down and swept his tongue up Samantha's slit. He felt her wetness on his tongue, and it was all he could do not to tear into her. The taste on his tongue was sweeter than the first drop of blood he ever took. With a growl, he swooped down and licked her slit from bottom to top, relishing every drop of her essence. He couldn't get enough, and with his fingers spread her wide open and used his tongue to lick every spot he could find to taste the sweet nectar. Samantha was bucking and thrashing and moaning, but Eduardo hardly paid attention.

"More," was all he could say between swipes of his tongue. When his tongue swept over the swollen little nub he was rewarded with more. He growled and licked and went back to the nub to suckle it until he got what he wanted.

Unexpectedly Samantha yelled out and he felt the pulsations begin. Sweet heaven, she was going to come. In. His. Mouth.

In anticipation, Eduardo's tongue began long, broad motions, and a second later he was rewarded by her sweet juices. In a frenzy of need he lapped up every drop. His cock was throbbing, and without word or thought he grabbed it and guided it into her opening.

"Yessss.... Your hole fits so tightly around my cock," he moaned.

"Good God, Eduardo. Harder…please."

Eduardo pumped his hips hard and fast, and when Samantha moaned, "I'm going to come…," he pounded once, twice, and felt her muscles tightening. He pulled out and caught the flood of juices in his mouth. With a roar he slammed back into her and lifted her legs to go deeper. He pumped hard a few times and felt his come shoot into her.

"Ahhhh…fuck…."

He collapsed on top of her, and hearing her grunt rolled them onto their sides. His eyes were closed, and when he opened them he looked into a pair of brown eyes that held amazement and awe.

"That was the best oral I've ever had."

Eduardo's eyes held the same awe as he stared back at her. "More?"

Chapter 15

Samantha had found heaven. The vampire that was at the moment between her widely spread thighs had the most amazing tongue. It was not only long, but also wide. It also seemed to have strength. When he lapped at her folds it caused her to dig her hands into the mattress underneath her to anchor her body so she wouldn't move away from that wonderful mouth.

Eduardo suckled on her throbbing clit and pushed two fingers inside her.

"Oh yes, Eduardo. Don't stop!" She screamed. She was trying to hold on, but when his tongue wiggled its way inside her along side of the two fingers still pumping in and out, she exploded. Her head thrashed back and forth while he continued to milk every drop from her throbbing cunt.

When she at last stilled Eduardo crawled up her body.

"*Dio*! Samantha, are you okay?" Eduardo asked as he brushed tears from her face.

"Yes...," she managed in a whisper. "It was so amazing. I can't believe that I've lived thirty-two years without that, without your tongue and mouth."

Eduardo looked at her intently, as if he wanted to tell her something.

Taking his face in her hands she said, "What is it, Eduardo?"

"You were the first woman I've ever tasted," he confessed.

Shocked, she asked, "How is that possible? You're a vampire. You must be old. In all those years a woman never asked you to do that?"

Eduardo sighed. "I am almost 175 years old. I became vampire at the age of twenty-five. My family was influential and wealthy. Women had always thrown themselves at me, ready to do anything I desired. When I became vampire, nothing changed except that there were more women who were drawn to my vampire allure. I'm not being conceited, but they were always so grateful to be in my bed that they never asked for anything from me. In my mind I was entitled to let them pleasure me."

Samantha squirmed on the bed and Eduardo said with no small amount of disgust, "You think me shallow and vain. You're right, I am. I never think about anyone besides myself."

He made to move off the bed, but Samantha grabbed his arm. "It's not that Eduardo. It's just that…that you described me."

She looked down in embarrassment. "Five years ago my husband left me. He told me that I was cold. That fucking me was like fucking a mannequin."

Eduardo swore and Samantha quickly cut him off. "He was right. I couldn't have an orgasm. I tried to make it up to him by giving him hours of blow jobs and every fantasy he had ever entertained. But in the end it wasn't enough for him. He left and I didn't blame him."

"Samantha, none of that makes you vain or shallow," Eduardo said, confused.

"That's where it started. Ever since I hit puberty, I had a body that would turn every man's head no matter his age. When I was a teenager I learned to wear clothes that hid my curves. When my husband left me, I decided that it was time to stop hiding my assets and use them to my advantage.

"The first few months, I had many offers and took a few men to my bed. But it was always the same. I could see the disappointment in their faces as I tried to fake an orgasm.

"It was around that time that I was recruited by the UGA. They had seen some research I'd done on animal behavior. Not having much else going for me, I joined and my first assignment was in Africa. There was a researcher there named Baruti who kept asking me out. I finally agreed and went out with him. I wanted to be honest about my sexual inadequacies so I told him about it. He looked at me for a long minute and said, "You just haven't had the right stimulation. Let me try and make you come, Samantha." We went back to his place. I really didn't have much hope that this time would be different."

Her eyes got a dreamy expression. "But I was wrong, it was different. He kissed me and it was nice. His mouth moved to my neck, trailing kisses downward. When he spread my thighs wide, I tried to stop him. No one had ever done that to me. It seemed too personal, but Baruti promised he would stop if I didn't like it. At the first touch of his tongue along my slit, I bucked off the bed and came hard. That night I had many orgasms, both from him going down on me and him fucking me. It was as if my sexuality had finally come alive.

"From that day on, I took control. If a man didn't perform to my liking I would kick him out of my bed. It became all about my pleasure and all about me."

Eduardo smiled at her. "We are like two peas in a pod, I'd say."

Samantha smiled back. "I signed up for this assignment thinking that a vampire would have had years to hone his oral skills."

Eduardo looked away. "I'm sorry I disappointed you. It would have been better for you to pick one of the other men."

Samantha pulled his face back towards her. "Oh Eduardo, I'm not disappointed. You're a quick learner, and I'd be honored if you practice on me."

And then Samantha did something she hadn't in a long time. She went down on him.

Chapter 16

Liam watched the others being paired off. He already knew which lass was going to claim him. A pretty redhead kept shooting glances his way. He had made eye contact once and smiled at the lass, but her cheeks had turned red and she had quickly looked away. Liam loved the shy ones.

He thought back to his days in Kerry as a young lad before he had been turned vampire. In the 1700's Kerry had been a small fishing village, and he had worked on his father's boat. The buxom maids would walk by while he hauled the day's catch to the icehouse. He knew they liked to watch his muscles bulge under his heavy burden. During the summer he would remove his shirt so he could get them good and worked up. In the evenings, after cleaning up he would go back to the village and persuade the shy lasses to give him kisses.

Now, some three hundred years later, he still attracted the shy ones. He credited it to his easygoing nature. Liam had always been quick to smile, and even quicker to laugh. Of course, his black curly hair, grey eyes and most of all, the bulging muscles didn't hurt either.

Liam felt for the poor, shy woman and made his way to where she sat.

"Hi, my name is Liam. Do you mind if I sit by you a little while then?"

The woman, whose face was bright red, just nodded.

"And what might your name be, lass?"

She tried clearing her throat. "Barr..bb. Barbara."

"Well, hello then Barbara. It's very nice to meet you."

Liam took her hand and her eyes bugged out. He laughed.

"Barbara, stop looking as if I'm going to swallow you whole. I don't bite." With a wink he added, "Unless of course you want me to."

Barbara's eyes went wide and her breathing quickened. Liam could smell her desire and his cock jumped in anticipation.

"Let's get out of here, lass."

He didn't wait for an answer from her. He grabbed her hand and led her out and down the hall to his quarters. He could feel her hand trembling in his and grinned with the thought of his sweet, slow seduction of the shy woman.

As he ushered her into his quarters, he knew that he had to go slow.

"Why don't we sit down?" He said, sweeping his hand to indicate the table and two chairs in the corner. He would rather be on the bed, but he didn't want to scare her off.

She smiled at him shyly and took a seat in one of the chairs. He made some small talk about his life in Kerry before he was a vampire, not wanting to remind her of that with her skittishness.

After about twenty minutes of his talking and her nodding, he'd had enough. He had a job to do…seduce the woman and make her fall under his charms. Besides, he was beginning to think that this one was hopeless. He sensed her desire, but not once had he received any other indication that she wanted to fuck him.

There was an awkward moment of silence. He searched his brain, trying to think of a move that wouldn't freak her out.

"Spank me."

Liam's head snapped up. "Pardon me?"

"Spank me."

Liam stared at her like an idiot. He knew that he could not have heard her just ask for a spanking.

"What did you say?"

"Spank me."

Liam put his hand over his mouth because he was sure it was hanging open. Spank her? What the fuck?

He cleared his throat. "You want me to spank you?"

"Yes."

"Ahhh…do you like that sort of thing?"

"Oh yes."

Liam ran a hand through his hair. He wasn't really into that, but he couldn't see how he could get out of it. He had a job to do.

He smiled at her. "Sure lass, whatever you want."

She got a big grin on her face. What he had been looking forward to before, he now looked on without much enthusiasm. He stood and pulled her to her feet. Holding her hand, he walked over to stand in front of the bed. She just stood there, so he leaned down and kissed her. Her lips were soft and sweet, and he again felt his cock jump. He deepened the kiss and used his tongue to part her lips. She wrapped her arms around his neck and pressed her body close.

"Now that's a sweet lass," he murmured.

"Spank me."

Jesus Christ! Was that all this woman could say? Fine, he would spank her then. He doubted he would be able to fuck her, because once again his hard on was lost.

He sat down on the bed and pulled her over his knee, but she resisted. Standing up, she unzipped her pants and slid them down her long shapely legs. His gaze stopped on her thatch of red curls. He licked his lips. Maybe he'd be able to fuck her after all.

Barbara smiled and placed herself over his knee once again, presenting her smooth white bottom. He swallowed hard. Her ass was a piece of art. He ran his hand over the two cheeks, his finger tracing the cleft. He realized that his cock was now hard as a rock and throbbing. He let his hand trail the cleft until it went all the way around to those red curls he had admired. His fingers rubbed along her slit and couldn't wait to feel her slick wetness. Except there was no wetness. Barbara clearly was not as excited as he was.

"What's the matter lass? Doesn't this feel good?"

"Spank me."

Liam closed his eyes, this time to try and control his anger. What the hell was wrong with this woman? He heard her sigh as if she was bored, and he saw red.

He brought his hand up in the air. CRACK. There, he had spanked her. He saw the red hand print on the smooth white of her ass and he immediately felt bad.

"I'm sorry, lass."

"Again."

He realized that she was moaning...and not in a bad way, but in a turned on kind of way.

What the hell? He thought as he brought his hand down on her bottom again. This time she moaned loudly and began to squirm with need. Her moans sent a bolt of electricity straight to his balls. Over and over he spanked her bottom. His arousal was unbelievable. Each time his hand came down on her ass, she writhed and moaned and he felt the tightening in his balls. He didn't even realize he was moaning too. He lifted his hand and spanked her hard.

"I'm coming," she cried out, and indeed when his hand slid down and around her ass, he felt the wetness seeping out of her. He couldn't resist thrusting two fingers into her cunt and cried out when she pumped her hips against them. He felt her shudder and he couldn't take it anymore.

"Inside you."

He threw her back on the bed and opened his pants. As his cock sprung free he let out a hiss. He couldn't remember ever being so hot and hard before. He was afraid he would come after two pumps inside this woman.

He entered her fast but stopped when he was buried deep. He tried to slow his breathing. If he moved even an inch he was going to shoot his load.

Barbara pushed on his shoulders, and with a groan he rolled them over so she was on top.

"Give me a second," he asked in a hoarse voice.

Her hips stayed still but she guided his hands, which were gripping her hips, and moved them to her ass.

His heartbeat quickened when he realized what she wanted. He slapped her ass hard, and she threw her head back and began to ride him. He bucked against her and gave her ass another slap. She went wild. With every slap he cried out as she did, and this time he shouted, "I can't hold it, I'm gonna come."

He came in hot spurts that seemed to go on and on. Having found her own release, she sagged against his chest.

Liam swept her soft red curls behind her ear and smiled at her. This shy woman had taught him something that he had never known in his three hundred years. Spanking got him off big time. He kissed her soft mouth and whispered, "Spank me."

Jude Stephens

Chapter 17

Barbara watched Liam as he tied her ankles and hands to the bedpost. She was so turned on. She loved being in the submissive role. Her late husband Sean had enjoyed playing these games. She wished she had some of her toys with her. She had not used them since his death a year and half ago.

Liam kept glancing at her with eyes blazing. When she was secure he knelt beside the bed and asked her, "Okay lass, you're helpless. What now? I'm rather new at this stuff."

"Now you use my body any way you want, and you use it hard."

Liam groaned. "Oh lass, you're putting naughty thoughts in my mind."

Barbara shivered. This was what she wanted, what she hoped for when she signed up for this assignment. She wanted a vicious, unscrupulous vampire to use her as a sex slave.

"Turn your naughty thoughts into reality, Vampire. Let your instincts take over."

"Are you sure, lass? I don't want to hurt you."

"I'm sure. Use my body for your pleasure and it will bring me pleasure too."

Liam leaned down and gave her a soft kiss. "That will be the last soft thing you get from me for awhile."

Barbara groaned, his words causing a rush of liquid to spill from her throbbing pussy.

"I smell your arousal, lass. I bet you're wet for me, aren't you?"

He was kneeling on the bed between her spread legs, his cock hard and jutting forward. He swept his fingers through her slick folds and brought the sweet moisture back to his cock and started stroking it. He was using slow, long pulls, and when he reached the tip he would use two fingers to squeeze and massage the red throbbing head.

Barbara squirmed, her pussy aching. She drew in a ragged breath when his other hand reached down and lifted his heavy sac. He rolled his balls in his hand and a low moan escaped him.

She was so hot and she couldn't stop from saying "Please...."

"Ahhh, lass. Are you aching for some of this?"

Barbara couldn't speak, was only able to nod yes.

She watched as he crawled up her body and, straddling her abdomen, brought his cock close to her mouth. There was a drop of pre-cum glistening on the thick head.

"Lick it," he commanded.

With the tip of her tongue she reached out and licked if off. The taste of him sent tingles down her spine, and she started lapping at his cock.

"Now lass," he rasped as he pulled away from her. He moved up a little further. "Lick my balls."

Barbara licked him with long sweeps of her tongue, and then took him into her mouth and sucked softly.

"Ahhh God...woman." Liam groaned as he held onto the headboard with one hand while the other was fisted around his cock, jerking off. He suddenly pulled back.

Barbara nearly came from the heat in his eyes.

"I told you to lick and instead you sucked. You need to learn obedience."

Her body shook with anticipation. He took a hardened nipple between two fingers and rolled it gently while blowing a cooling breath over it.

Barbara moaned and he looked up at her. "Do you like that, lass?" She nodded and he smiled seductively.

"How about this?"

He pinched the nipple hard while giving it a little twist. Barbara bucked her body off the bed and cried out, "Yesssss…. Oh yessss…."

Her reaction enticed him, and with a growl, Liam moved back down between her spread legs. He spread the lips of her pussy wide and found her clit. He alternated stroking it with his tongue and his fangs. Barbara thought she would surely die from the pleasure-pain. She'd never felt something so wonderfully balanced before.

She felt her climax building and couldn't hold back. She screamed with her release, "Oh God, Liam…yesss…."

Her explosion set him off and with a roar, he positioned himself on top of her, and while her pussy was still in the throes of her orgasm, he plunged his cock into her and sank his fangs into her neck.

Barbara had never felt anything like it before. The pleasure of his cock pounding in and out of her was exquisite, and the hot, searing pain with each mouthful of blood he sucked out of her neck was the ultimate in contrasting sensations. She was aware that she was moaning, and felt a tear trickle down her face. She felt like she had left her body and was in another dimension, where sensations were magnified a thousand times.

Liam slammed into her and with no warning he came. His fangs slid out of Barbara's neck, his head jerked back, and he roared.

Barbara became aware of his weight on top of her. She wasn't sure if she had passed out, but if she did it hadn't been for long. She felt his cock still twitching inside her, along with her muscles contracting in response.

Liam must have come back to himself too, because after untying her, he rolled them onto their sides, though he didn't pull out of her body.

They both groaned when the motion caused an aftershock of pleasure.

"Lass, I don't know what to say. I'm sorry I bit you. I don't know what you do to me. You make me lose all control."

Barbara placed her hands on either side of his face. "Don't be sorry about biting me. It was incredible. That is what this is all about. Giving and receiving pleasure. The pain is a necessary part in my receiving pleasure. You said you didn't know what to do, but you did. It was instinctive on your part and you're very, very good at it."

He laughed. "So are you, lass. After we rest do you think you'd get off by tying me to the bed?"

Barbara pictured Liam tied to the bed and a bolt of lust shot through her body. He must have felt it too because the laughter died on his lips and his eyes turned molten. She felt him hardening inside of her.

"I think the possibility is good."

Chapter 18

Blayze watched the woman through narrowed eyes. She was toying with him. She was exquisite, tall and lithe. Her chestnut brown hair was gathered in an elegant chignon. She was dressed in Gucci, carmel colored slacks and sable brown silk shirt. Blayze knew it was from their fall collection. He did after all, live in Paris. He also had an eye for a well dressed woman. Blayze appreciated beauty like no other. He was seldom without a supermodel on his arm.

Women, like the one before him, all played the same game. They were as jaded as he was with too much money, too much alcohol, and too much promiscuous sex. The only thing they lacked was immortality, and at the moment his was in jeopardy. He needed to get on with seducing this woman. She would be a challenge to deceive because they both had the same character flaws, but he loved nothing more than a challenge.

Having run out of patience, Blayze walked across the room and confronted the woman.

"Excuse me for being so forward, but my name is Blayze and I couldn't help but admire you from across the room."

"You couldn't help it? Are you telling me that you were trying not to admire me?"

Blayze was taken aback at her quick wit, and his eyebrows rose further when she smiled at him. It was a genuine smile that lit up her brown eyes.

"I'm sorry; I shouldn't tease you like that when you just introduced yourself. Hi, my name is Diane."

Blayze stared at the hand that she offered for a second before he brought it to his lips to kiss. This woman was confusing him.

"Hello Diane. Do not apologize. I appreciate a quick wit. Would you care to join me this evening?"

"You cut to the chase, don't you? Well, seeing as we both know why we're here, we might as well."

Again Blayze's eyebrows rose. This woman was an enigma. He could swear that he recognized the cool indifference of a jaded individual, yet he saw flashes of genuine emotions.

They walked to his quarters in silence, though it wasn't an uncomfortable silence. Blayze opened the door and allowed her to enter first.

"I apologize for the lack of amenities."

"It's fine, though this must be difficult for you. You seem like a man who is used to the finer things in life."

Blayze was surprised by her understanding and almost sympathetic attitude. This might be easier than he thought, especially if she sympathized with their plight.

"Yes, I am. I do miss my penthouse and the view of Paris at night…it's quite lovely."

Unbidden, Blayze thought of the rags he once wore, the smell of death and rotting corpses, and the constant pain of hunger.

"Are you all right?" Diane said at his side with her hand on his arm.

"I'm sorry, I got lost in reminiscing about the beauty of Paris, when I should be basking in the beauty before me. Please make yourself comfortable."

Diane gave him a hard glance, but sat on the edge of the bed with her ankles delicately crossed. Blayze went over to a small control panel on the wall and pushed a button. Piped in music began to play.

"It's not Chopin, but it's music."

As one song ended another began. "Muskrat Love."

A look of horror passed over Blayze's face. "Good Lord, what is that?"

Diane laughed, and Blayze's blood heated at the rich warm sound. Without realizing it he was standing before her, holding out his hand.

Her laughter stopped, but the warmth from it still sparkled in her eyes. She put her hand in his and he pulled her up and into his arms. He held her for a brief second before he began to sway to the music. As he held her close, Blayze felt an unusual desire for this woman, but there was something else that he couldn't describe. It felt as if he were content, but since he hadn't felt that way in a long time he dismissed it.

Blayze didn't want the moment to end. He was enjoying the feel of this woman in his arms. Her head was on his shoulder, and he almost jumped when he felt soft lips on his neck. He kept swaying to the music, because for the life of him he didn't want her to stop.

Her lips trailed soft kisses up his neck to his ear, where she nibbled and almost caused his knees to buckle. When her tongue began a journey along his jaw he actually moaned. Her tongue found his lips and they parted as it slipped inside his mouth. He couldn't remember ever being kissed like this. It was soft and sensual. Their tongues did a slow erotic dance, and when Diane pulled back he wanted to cry out at the loss.

She led him over to stand by the bed. She stared at him as she began unbuttoning her blouse. He stared back as he undid the buttons on his shirt. Their eyes never left each other as they undressed at a slow pace. Blayze was shaking inside. He had never been so affected by a woman before.

She turned as she took off her lacy bra and quickly pulled him down to the bed on top of her. He rained soft kisses over her face, and then captured her mouth in a kiss that was so sensual that they both were writhing. Their bodies slid against each other to arouse them further. Blayze grabbed her hand and entwined their fingers. He broke the kiss and began to trail kisses down her neck to her collarbone on his way to capture her breast.

He froze. His eyes went to hers. They were shining bright. Something deep inside him shattered. He slowly lowered his head but kept his eyes locked with hers, and slowly laved the hardened nipple. He moved to the other breast and did the same. When she parted her thighs, he positioned himself at her entrance. He took his cock in his hand and rubbed it along her slit. She was wet and ready for him. He groaned at the way her soft wet folds felt against him. The look in her eye turned pleading and he could not deny her.

He entered her slowly so that he could relish every second this first time. He had no doubt this would be the first of many. When he was fully buried in her tight warmth, it felt like heaven. He kissed her mouth and his tongue took up the slow sweet rhythm of his hips.

When Diane began moaning, the sweet sound nearly made him come. He groaned with the effort not to come until she did. Her kisses became frenzied and he knew she was close. Thank God, he thought.

His strokes became more urgent and she broke her mouth free of his and said, "I'm going to come."

He tenderly smoothed the hair from her face. "Let go, *mon amour*. I want you to come hard for me."

He felt her tightening around him and he pumped into her hard. He threw his head back as his climax hit without warning at the same moment as hers. They both cried out. His seed came in long, hot spurts even after Diane had gone limp.

"I'm sorry," he rasped as he continued to thrust into her.

"It's okay, don't stop."

"I can't stop...it feels so good."

She wrapped her arms around him and held him tight. He pumped and ground his pelvis hard into hers as his come kept spilling forth. He cried out, "Ahhhhh…yesssss," when he felt one last big ejaculation. Feeling drained, literally, he slid out of her and fell beside her. "*Merde*. I have never come like that before." He rolled onto his side to look at her. "I feel like a fool asking this, but I have to. Have you ever made love like that before?"

She smiled sweetly at him. "No, never. I thought that maybe that's the way it always is with vampires."

"And I thought that was the way it always is with you."

Blayze gathered her into his arms, and she snuggled against him and closed her eyes. A few minutes later, her even breathing told him that she was sleeping.

He lay there for a long time staring at the ceiling, making his plans.

Chapter 19

Diane awoke and found Blayze staring at her. His face was drawn in confusion. She knew what he was thinking. He had seen the scars.

"Five years ago, I was diagnosed with breast cancer. I went through chemotherapy and beat it. And then two months ago, I found out it returned."

Blayze smoothed the hair from her brow. "Have you started treatments again?"

"No. I'm not doing anything this time. I can't go through that again."

"So, you're giving up?"

"No, I'm not giving up; I'm just not fighting it anymore. What will be will be."

"That sounds like giving up to me," he said softly.

Diane felt her anger rising. "What would you know? You're a vampire for Christ sakes...you're facing forever."

Blayze stood, and finding his silk boxers, slid them on and sat on the edge of the bed.

"I wasn't always a vampire, you know. Once I was a man, a man with a wife and two sons."

Diane watched as his eyes took on a sheen of unshed tears as his memories flashed before him. She was sure that whatever he was going to say was hard for him to talk about. She sat up and took his hand in her hers. He didn't seem to notice.

"Right after the onset of the revolution in France, there was a period now called the Reign of Terror. It lasted a year and one month. Anyone who was considered an enemy of the revolution was executed, usually by guillotine. A number of nobility were targeted, including me, though I was of minor consequence. I was Duke of Chartres, an insignificant lineage in the scheme of things. I had never even been to court.

"In an effort to save his own skin I was named as a major player in the efforts to quell the revolutionaries by the Duke of Mortemart. A man, by the way, I hardly knew. I was tipped off by a friend that they would be coming for me to execute me. My wife, Brielle, was adamant that I flee. I wanted to take her and the boys with me, but she was correct that it would most likely put them in even more danger. The streets of Paris were no place for women and children.

"I lived on the Paris streets for nine months. I only got to see my family sporadically, as it was too dangerous to go back often. We had a small network of nobility who exchanged information about our families and friends. It was here that I found out that my wife and sons had been beheaded."

Diane, with tears streaming down her face, wrapped her arms around this man who she had, at first glance, thought a cold and calculating male.

He wrapped his arms around her and rocked them back and forth as he continued.

"My sons were only three and five years old. As the days dragged on, I couldn't stop picturing them in my mind. One night as I lay in a dark, stinking back alley, I found a sharp piece of glass and slit my wrists. As my lifeblood ran out, I felt warm and at peace. But I awoke two days later, a vampire. It seems a vampire was drawn by the scent of my blood and decided to keep me. I hated her for bringing me back, and as soon as I could, I left her."

Diane stiffened in his arms when he said, "That is why I'm giving you a choice."

"You want to turn me vampire?"

"I will try and turn you vampire if you want me to. It is a risk. Not all humans survive the process. I will have to drain all of your blood and replace it with mine."

Diane had never given the possibility a thought. Even when she took this assignment she had only hoped to experience something new. To live and feel before it was too late.

Then the vampire said the one thing that made up her mind.

"Don't give up. For some reason, I don't want you to. You've made me feel alive for the first time since I woke up a vampire."

Diane pulled back and looked at him. His face was a mask of granite, but his eyes shone with a vulnerability that melted her heart.

"When do we start?"

Chapter 20

Soren watched as Blayze left with his woman. That meant that there was one woman left. The one he would fuck and eventually kill. He'd remained towards the back of the room all evening, not conversing with anyone. A few women looked his way, drawn by his short blond hair, blue eyes, and chiseled good looks, but they quickly turned away when they saw the fierce look in his eyes.

He hadn't paid much attention to the people around him, and he had no idea what woman remained for him. Not that it mattered. Despite Nicholas's worries about him, he would do whatever was necessary to get out of this hellhole. He'd been here ten months now and not one single day had gone by that he didn't think about the ways he would kill those responsible for his brother Peder's death.

Soren stood and looked around. What the hell? He didn't see anyone in the room. Oh hell no, one of those vampires did not leave with two women.

"Fuck!"

His head snapped to a corner to his right when he heard a small gasp. Moving in that direction, he saw a slight figure curled up in a chair in the corner.

It was a woman...at least he thought it was. Her head was bent, staring at a book that was sitting in her lap. Her long brown hair hung down, shielding her face from him.

"Hello." Recognizing that he sounded rough and impatient, he tried again. He needed her trust, for a little while anyway. "My name is Soren. I guess you've been waiting for me. I'm sorry I didn't see you sitting here before."

She looked up from her book, and Soren was surprised to see how young she was. She couldn't be more than twenty.

She pushed a pair of tortoise shell glasses up the bridge of her nose.

"Um. Hi."

Soren held back a groan. He didn't know if seducing this slip of a girl would be easy or hard. On one hand, she may have years of suppressed hormones raging inside of her. On the other hand, she may be too skittish to enjoy sex. He tried to hide his aggravation.

"Well, since we're the last two left, we might as well go back to my quarters where we'll be more comfortable."

He didn't know if he'd be upset or relieved if she refused. He raised an eyebrow in surprise as she didn't hesitate, but hastily got to her feet, letting her book drop. They both bent to retrieve the book and ended up butting heads.

"Sorry," she mumbled.

"No problem." This was not good. How was he supposed to have sex with this woman when he wasn't the least bit attracted to her?

She hastily retrieved the book and headed for the door. He almost had to run to catch up with her. He grabbed her arm as she turned down the hall in the wrong direction. He was beginning to think he knew why she volunteered for this assignment. She just wasn't too bright.

Soren opened the door to his room and ushered her inside. The girl took a few steps inside and stood there, hugging her book to her chest.

Christ! Soren thought to himself. How the hell does a man seduce a girl like this? He had never had a problem seducing women before. Over the years he and his brother had made a sort of game of it. Whenever they would go out drinking, they would see who could get the most beautiful woman in the bar to go home with him. He smiled when he thought how his brother Peder had always managed to charm the pants off women. Literally.

His smiled faded as he thought about Peder lying in this hell hole slowly dying. He would seduce this girl, and then he would take pleasure watching as he slowly drained the life from her.

"Make yourself comfortable. Would you like a drink or something Miss...I don't think you told me your name."

"My name is Sparkle, and I'm fine, thank you."

Sparkle? Soren thought he had never seen anyone less suited to their name than this mousy, shy girl in front of him.

"Okay Sparkle. Let's sit down and get to know each other better."

He went over to the bed and sat down, and watched as she went over to the small table and sat in one of the two chairs. Frustration made him run an agitated hand through his short blond hair.

Getting up, he went over and sat in the other chair.

"So how old are you, Sparkle? You look young."

"I'm twenty-five."

"Well, that is young, compared to my age."

For the first time Sparkle's eyes lit up, and Soren could understand why she was named Sparkle. Her eyes were a golden color and lit up with her excitement.

"How old are you?" She asked excitedly.

"I was born in 1893."

She was staring at him with awe. Soren smiled. Now he knew her weakness and knew how to seduce the whore.

He began talking about the things he'd seen over the last hundred years, and was pleased to notice that she had loosened up and had even set her damn book on the table. When he thought that she was more comfortable with him he said, "Why don't we move over to the bed and get more comfortable?"

Her eyes widened and filled with panic. "I...um...I have some Uno cards in my purse. Maybe we can play Uno for awhile."

"Uno? Is that one of those naughty party games?"

"No. It's a regular card game that you play and has numbers and colors and you have to...."

Soren tuned her blathering out as he stood, grabbed her hand, and pulled her over to the bed. He'd had enough. He had a job to do.

He pulled her down to sit next to him on the edge of the bed.

"Enough about Uno, Sparkle. Don't be afraid of me. I only want to please you."

Soren lifted his hand and stroked her long brown hair. It was amazingly soft and silky.

"Let me show you how good I can make you feel."

He leaned in and placed his lips against hers. Her lips were pursed tightly together, but he refused to stop. His tongue came out and traced her soft, full lips, and he thought that her mouth was made for kissing if she would just loosen up. He continued his assault and nibbled on her bottom lip until he heard her moan and her mouth parted slightly. Going slowly, so as not to frighten her, he slipped his tongue into her mouth. She tasted like honey, and he couldn't help but deepen the kiss. He held her head between his hands and slanted his mouth over hers. His tongue probed and swirled around hers until finally, with a moan, she tentatively moved her tongue against his.

"Oh yeah, baby...that's it," he murmured against her mouth.

He guided her back so she was laying flat on the bed, never taking his mouth from hers. He trailed his hand from her hair down her neck over her collar bone to the swell of her breast.

He felt her stiffen and he moved his hand back up to her hair and continued kissing her, even though his hand was itching to retreat to her breast. He was pleasantly surprised that her breasts were full and firm. He needed to find the thing that made her go over the edge. Thinking back to how excited she had been to hear about his life as a vampire, an idea came to him.

Kissing her, he began to writhe and moan. It must have excited her a little because she unknowingly began to move her hips slightly. For the first time Soren felt his blood begin to stir, but he would need more for his plan to work. He started thrusting his hips, hoping she wouldn't notice that he had no erection.

Pretending to be overcome with lust, he broke away from her.

"I'm sorry...I can't help...the need is great," he panted.

Sparkle turned to him and gasped when she saw his fangs. He thought it would be a nice touch in his little production.

"May I touch them?"

Hell! He had thought she would get a little turned on by the seeing the vampire in him. Instead she was looking at him like a science project.

"Sure."

Sparkle's index finger traced down the length of one fang and at the same time she was peering into his mouth, trying to get a good look. He wondered if she was a dentist.

"Ow!" Sparkle pulled her finger back and put it in her mouth.

Soren felt a powerful jolt from the drop of blood that fell on his tongue. Desire swept through him and he felt his cock spring to life.

He couldn't seem to stop himself when he pulled Sparkle's finger out of her mouth and put it in his. The taste of her blood was like pure lust pouring into him with each pull he took.

He also couldn't stop the moans that erupted from deep in his chest. Unconsciously, his hand travelled down and he was stroking his rock hard cock through his jeans.

He locked eyes with Sparkle and her eyes widened and he smelled her arousal.

His hands moved to open her pants.

"Are you wet and ready for me, baby? Your blood is so sweet; I can't wait to taste you. I want to lick and drink every drop when you come in my mouth."

She tried to grab his hands as he slid her pants and her panties down in one quick movement, but he didn't even notice. All he could think about was tasting her.

Moving down, he grabbed her legs and spread them wide. His head moved in close and her scent made him dizzy. He swiped his tongue up her slit and they both cried out. She tasted like manna from heaven, and his tongue, in a frenzy of need, began swirling through every fold, probing every inch. His mouth found her clit and he sucked hard while he inserted two fingers into her opening. He felt her body trembling and he groaned.

"Yes baby...come for me. Let me taste your sweet cream. That's it...give it to me."

"Ahhh!" She screamed and bucked as she came.

His tongue made sure he got every creamy drop.

"Soren!" She yelled as she came again.

Soren stiffened when she yelled his name. The sound of his name in her husky, sexy voice was making him climax. What the fuck? He couldn't hold it back as hard as he tried. He felt it like hot lava moving from his balls up to his throbbing cock. He couldn't come yet. He had to fuck her.

Gritting his teeth, he took off his pants. He moaned as his aching cock sprang free. He guided it to her entrance and plunged into her in one swift motion.

Sparkle cried out in pain.

Soren froze. No way. He turned Sparkle's face towards him and saw the tears.

"Sparkle? Why didn't you say something?"

"I…I was afraid to."

Soren closed his eyes. The whore was a virgin. He started to pull his still hard cock out of her.

"Please, don't stop. I wasn't afraid of you. I was afraid you wouldn't want me," she said softly.

"If you'd told me I would have gone easy. I can't believe that I took you so roughly. I'm sorry Sparkle."

And the strange thing was that he truly was sorry. This woman was amazingly brave to come here a virgin, and sacrifice that to save a vampire, someone different and frightening to her. He looked at her again, though this time he saw her beautiful, intelligent gold eyes and her soft pink lips. He began to move his hips slowly.

"I promise you that you'll feel only pleasure, baby. Does this feel good?" He asked as he slid almost all the way out and inched back in.

"Yessss…," she moaned.

"How about this?" He asked as he swiveled his hips, touching her sensitive core.

"God yessss…."

He smiled and reached down and softly rubbed her clit. His smile faded as she arched her back off the bed, taking his cock deeper.

"Fuck that felt good," he groaned. She did it again.

"Sparkle, you have to stop that. You're going to make me come," he ground out between gritted teeth. "Fuckkk!" He roared when she did it again. "Dammit woman. I'm trying to go slow and give you pleasure, and you're making me want to rip in to you."

She reached up and grabbed his head so he would look at her.

"So rip into me then. I want you to. I'm okay. The pain is gone, and all I feel is this wild need and I don't know what to do. Teach me, Soren."

Something inside him shifted as he looked at the woman under him. He swallowed. He didn't have a choice anymore. With a primitive growl he lifted her legs and pumped his cock into her hard and fast. She screamed and it only incited him further. He changed position so he was kneeling and he almost lost it as he watched his red, glistening cock sliding in and out of her. He wanted to see her tits, so he wrapped his arms around her and rolled them over.

"Ride me, baby," he moaned.

"How?" She gasped as he bucked his hips up.

He grabbed her hips and guided her. It didn't take long for her to pick up a maddening rhythm.

"Take off your shirt," he commanded.

Never slowing her ride on his cock, she pulled her shirt over her head and without being asked undid her bra.

Soren hissed when saw her tits. They were larger than he thought they'd be, with dark, dusky nipples that were standing at hard points.

He reached up to tug at her nipples, but she swiped his hands away.

"Now this I'm good at," she said seductively.

Soren's mouth hung open as he watched her pull and twist her nipples with her head thrown back in pleasure.

"God, Sparkle. That is so hot. I want to come on your tits as you do that."

She cried out at his words and he knew that she was close.

"Do you play with yourself a lot?"

"Uh huh…."

"Oh God… I like watching you…how can a virgin be so fucking hot?"

She looked at him and he thought he would come just from the fire in her eyes.

"I may have been untouched by a man, but I was not untouched. I make myself orgasm at least twice a day. If I don't, I'll ache and throb between my legs all day."

Soren was breathless as he said, "God...I love it...you're so fucking hot. I bet you're gonna like it rough, aren't you?"

She cried out...and began riding him harder.

"I want to take you fast and hard against the wall."

She moaned and her hand moved between her legs.

"I'll fuck you so hard that your head will bang against the wall."

She rubbed her clit faster.

"I'll throw you on the floor and mount you from behind, and fuck you hard as my balls slap your luscious ass."

"YESSSS...." She screamed at the same time he did.

Soren's seed came out in hot spurts and he felt tingles move up his spine with every burst. He felt her muscles pulling and milking every last drop from him.

Shit! What the hell just happened? He thought. That was without a doubt the best sex he'd ever had. The shy little mouse had turned into a wildcat. As he lifted her off him and wrapped her in his arms, he thought there was a big difference between killing a mouse and a wildcat.

Chapter 21

Sparkle was sore. She got up to go to the bathroom and she could barely walk.

"Damn…I'm sorry Sparkle," Soren said as he got up, scooped her up in his arms, and carried her to the bathroom.

She laughed. "I'm not. It's a really good kind of sore."

He looked at her for a long while, making her uncomfortable. She wondered if she had something in her teeth. It wouldn't be the first time.

"Is something wrong?" She asked him.

"No…yes…I don't know."

He sat down in a chair with her still in his arms. She reached up, and stroking his cheek said, "What is it, Soren? You're sorry you made love to me, aren't you? I see it in your face. It's okay that you took my virginity. I've always been awkward, and I thought this would be a good way to get rid of it. I could give you something you needed and you could give me something that no one else would want. I never thought that it might be something that you wouldn't want either. I'm so sorry. I'll get dressed and go."

Sparkle jumped off his lap, grabbed her clothes, and went in the bathroom. She felt like an idiot. She wondered why she'd thought this would work. Even a man who would die without sex didn't want her. She was mortified. She needed some time to get herself together.

"I'm going to take a quick shower and then I'll be out of your way!" She shouted before she turned on the water.

She stepped in and let the warm water run over her body. Tears gathered but she refused to let them fall. Why couldn't she accept that she was different? From the time she was five she knew it, her parents knew it, and the world knew it. Her mind was different than everyone else's. She couldn't turn it off. Formulas and mathematical equations ran through her head uninvited. Her IQ wasn't even recordable, it was that high. She had raced through school and at the age of fifteen had her doctorate in biochemistry and had obtained several other degrees along the way.

Many organizations had wanted her, but she chose UGA because she saw a possibility that she may one day have a chance at saving the world. Now, she wasn't so sure.

Being with Soren last night had changed her outlook. She didn't see vampires as a threat. She saw them as beings with the same hopes and desires as all of creation shares. Before coming here she'd read all the vampire files, and she knew that Soren had lost his brother here last year. She also pored over all of the clinical data collected over the years, and knew without a doubt that the vampires were lying about needing sex to survive.

Sparkle finished her shower and dressed. She may be young and inexperienced, but she wasn't dumb. She opened the bathroom door and saw Soren still sitting where she had left him. And he was still naked. She tried hard to ignore it but it caused her pulse to quicken and an ache between her legs. This was her goddamn curse. She had an overactive sex drive and none of the charms needed to attract the opposite sex to fulfill the demands. She needed to get out of here quickly and take care of the building heat.

"Listen Soren, I know everything, and I want you to know that I will help you guys anyway I can. My only condition is that I don't want to see anyone hurt." She made her way to the door. "You can just ask the guard to get me if you need anything. Bye."

She opened the door, but it was slammed shut before she could get out.

A gasp escaped her as her arm was grabbed and she was pulled backwards. She bumped into Soren's hard *naked* body.

"What do you mean that you know everything? Tell me what you think you know," he snarled.

She really wasn't scared. Well, maybe a little. She *was* turned on. She cleared her throat.

"I know that you don't need to have sex to survive the polar nights. I saw the research that was done and all of it points to it more likely being that your organs can't maximize the blood you drink without your regular sleep. So it would be my guess that you're planning to use the women to help you escape."

His eyes narrowed and the hand on her arm tightened painfully. Yet her gaze was on his left nipple. It was standing erect and she couldn't think beyond the fact that she wanted to bite him there. And then lick him. Her own nipples hardened in response and she pressed her thighs tightly together to try and ease the ache. It made it worse and she gasped, which Soren took as fear.

"Tell me what else you know."

She knew she shouldn't push him, but she desperately wanted to get away from him so she could relieve the building fire inside her.

"I know about your brother Peder, and I'm so sorry, Soren. What the UGA is doing here is wrong. I know this may not be of any comfort to you, but I swear that I will find a way to make them stop taking vampires. You have the same rights as any other species does to survive."

His eyes swept up and she saw the pain reflected there. "I just wish that I had a chance to see him one more time."

Wrapping her arms around him she said, "I know. I wish it was within my power to give you that." She held him for a minute until the rich scent of his skin became more than she could bear. She pulled away and, heading towards the door, said, "Remember, tell the guard if you need me for anything."

"Where are you going?"

"Back to my room. I've got to take care of…something," she mumbled.

"Let me help you."

She turned startled eyes towards him. "Help me with what?'

He walked closer. "With your arousal."

Her mouth hung open. How did he know?

Guessing her question, he said, "I smelled it. You became aroused when you walked out of the bathroom and looked at me."

Her face flamed.

"When I put my hand on your arm it rose to the point where it made you wet."

Hearing him say it made her pussy clench and her panties damp.

He closed his eyes. "Right now your pussy is dripping and begging to be fucked."

She took a step back, but stopped herself. She really didn't want to be a pity fuck.

"It's okay. I really want to thank you for the earlier sex, but you don't need to help me. I can't impose on you like that."

"What are you taking about?"

"I'm talking about fucking me. It was great of you to do it before, but I don't want to put you out again. I can take care of my needs on my own."

"Are you insane?" He asked.

"Um...no....not that I'm aware of."

"Why do you think I wouldn't want to fuck you again?"

Hearing him say fuck you again made her groan. She really needed to get out of there before she did something stupid.

"Look at me! I'm not at all attractive. No one wants to fuck me. Strike that, no one has ever wanted to fuck me."

Soren rubbed his hand over his face. This woman-child standing in front of him had no idea how she made him feel. She was the most alluring female on the face of the earth. He wanted to lick her from head to toe and then fuck her for *days!*

Sparkle looked up when she heard him groan. Her eyes went wide when she saw his cock hard and standing up. Her legs were trembling.

"Christ, Sparkle stop...I will come if you don't," he pleaded.

She hadn't been aware that her fingers were tugging on her nipple through her blouse or that her other hand was rubbing her clit through her pants.

"Sorry...I gotta go," she mumbled.

"Like hell," he roared. He was in front of her, taking her clothes off. "You aren't going anywhere. Sparkle, it will kill me if you do. I've never desired another woman the way I desire you." Once naked, he backed her up against the door. "Your passion is just the icing on the cake. You're beautiful and you have no idea." He lifted her leg and trailed kisses up her calf. "You're smart and you're a gentle soul." He pushed his hard cock inside her. "You're good and honest." He pulled his cock almost all the way out and plunged it back in. She cried out and he said in a hoarse voice, "You're sexy." He pulled out again and plunged in hard. "You're hot." He pulled out until just the tip was inside her and slammed into her again. "You're so fucking tight."

When he pulled out again she grabbed his head and made him look at her. "Shut up and fuck me!"
And he did.

Chapter 22

Karen sat in her office going over paperwork. Or more exactly, updates from the pairings that had occurred three nights ago. She was pleased to see that things were going well. The women opted to stay with the men in their quarters each night.

She was supposed to meet with them yesterday, but had too many things to do and instead sent an assistant to interview both the vampires and the women volunteers.

Karen sighed. It wasn't true that she was too busy. She really didn't want to see Nicholas and his blonde bombshell Holly. She didn't know why she was acting so jealous. Nicholas had only kissed her once. Maybe it was because he made her ache in places where she thought she never would again.

She shook her head. She had to get rid of thoughts like that. She was a professional, for God's sake; she couldn't afford to get involved with a project on an intimate level. Doing so would get her fired, or worse, killed.

A knock on her door had her saying, "Come in."

"Sorry to interrupt you, Commander, but I have one of the women volunteers that desperately needs to speak with you."

"That's okay, Jenkins. Please show her in."

Karen watched as the blonde bombshell herself stepped into her office.

"Holly, what can I do for you?"

"I'm sorry to bother you, Commander, but I don't know what else to do."

At her tears, Karen handed her a box of tissues. "It's no bother. Now tell me why you're upset."

"It's Nicholas, the vampire that I'm...I'm with."

Karen stilled. "Has he hurt you?"

"NO! He hasn't hurt me. He hasn't done anything to me. That's the problem. I've failed my assignment."

Karen looked puzzled. "You mean he hasn't touched you?"

Holly's cheeks turned pink. "Well, he's touched me, but he hasn't had intercourse with me. All he does is use his mouth and fingers on me until I climax, and then for some reason I can't remember anything after that. I'm worried. If he doesn't have sex with someone he will die, and it will be my fault for not being able to attract him."

She began to cry and Karen went over and put her hand on her shoulder.

"Holly, the fault doesn't lie with you. Obviously, there's something wrong with the vampire." Karen didn't for a minute believe that, having seen evidence of his ability to perform.

"It must be me. It must be that I pass out after he...you know, makes me come. He can hardly have sex with someone who isn't strong enough for his lust."

She started crying again and Karen smoothed her hair back in a gesture of comfort and froze. On Holly's neck were two puncture marks. Trying to keep the anger out of her voice she said, "I'm sure that's not it. I'm going to have the medic prescribe you a mild sedative to help you relax. You'll stay in your own quarters until I've straightened this out."

Holly sniffed, "Thank you, Commander."

Karen called the medic, and after giving him instructions watched as he led Holly away.

Karen's eyes turned to steel as she made her way to Nicholas's quarters. Not bothering to knock, she opened the door and walked in. He was lying on the bed with his arms slung over his eyes, but jumped up when he heard the door slam closed. He didn't say anything, just stood there staring at her.

"What the hell do you think you're doing? Holly came to me and told me that you haven't had sex with her. Do you have a death wish or something?"

Nicholas ran an agitated hand through his hair. "No, I don't have a death wish, and I wouldn't exactly say that I didn't have sex with her either."

"Okay...we can squabble over what the term 'sexual relations' means, but that's been done before. I know that you've not penetrated her, and I also know that you've bitten her. We both know that is against the rules we set!" She was angry and breathing hard.

Karen's breathing accelerated even more when Nicholas stalked towards her until she was up against the wall.

Placing his hands on the wall on either side of her, he said in a low, menacing tone. "Do you want to know why I haven't fucked her? Because I haven't been able to. For the first time in my entire long existence, I can't get an erection."

Karen dragged her eyes from his burning gaze to his crotch, where his hard on was clearly defined in his jeans.

Following her gaze, he laughed bitterly. "Let me rephrase that. I can't get an erection for anyone but *you*. Do you know how many times I've gone into the bathroom after that twit Holly passed out and stroked myself as I thought about you? Six times. Six times I came into my own hand wishing it was your hand wrapped around my cock, your mouth licking and sucking me, your legs wrapped around my waist as I pounded the shit out of you."

Karen got scared at the fire that blazed out of control in his eyes.

"I should just fuck you now and get you the hell out of my system!"

"Fuck you...I'm not your fucking Viagra pill. It's not my fault you can't get it up."

She had no warning before he struck. He grabbed her hands and held them in his viselike grip above her head. His mouth came down hard against hers. She fought against kissing him back until his free hand grabbed her breast. Her mouth parted and she felt her hot juices flow from her pussy.

His tongue slipped into her mouth, and he kissed her long and deep while his fingers pinched her rigid nipple. His mouth moved along her jaw to her ear, and down the side of her neck.

"You don't know how often I've thought about doing just this. Having your soft skin beneath my lips, smelling your desire dampen your panties. I've never desired anyone the way I desire you. I ache to bury myself inside you."

Karen felt his whole body shudder and knew what it was costing him to hold back. She didn't know why but she believed his words. From the moment she had first glimpsed him she had felt a connection on another level. Whether it was lust or something else she didn't know, and didn't care. All she knew was that she would be a fool to ignore it.

"What are you waiting for?"

His head snapped up and he looked into her eyes and saw her need reflected in them. With a roar he tugged at her skirt as she tugged at his jeans. He ripped her panties off a second before she freed his cock from his jeans, and he wasted no time pushing into her.

They both cried out with the sensation. He thrust slow and hard, each thrust accompanied by a loud grunt.

"Fuck."

"Shit."

"Ahh...."

Her head and spine banged against the door with every thrust.

"You're so fucking tight and wet. You make me want to come already."

He continued his hard thrusts and clenched his jaw.

"Don't tell me that's all you got, Vampire."

She didn't know why she felt the need to incite him. She felt powerful in his need and lust for her.

"You're fucking asking for it now." He roared as he threw her on the floor face down, lifted her hips in the air, and plunged into her. "I'm going to make you beg me to let you come, but I won't until you're crazed with lust for me and what I only can give you. Ahhhh, fuck me," he cried out as Karen tightened her muscles around his cock and squeezed as tight as she could. He grabbed her hair. "So you think you can make me come before you, woman? You don't know what you've just started."

Letting go of her hair, he grabbed her hips and thrust into her with such force that Karen thought she'd buckle, and she did just that when he started moving his hips in a circular motion. His cock was sliding against a sensitive spot that sent waves of exquisite pleasure rolling though her whole body.

"You like that, don't you love? It makes you want to let go…let it fill and consume you. Come for me love…drench me with your come. I want to…ahhhh…."

He couldn't finish his words as Karen bucked back against each of his thrusts. Trying to gain the upper hand, he reached his hand between them and rubbed her swollen clit.

"Yeah…you're ready. You're so wet and your clit is throbbing. You'll come for me soon."

She lurched forward so fast that he had no time to stop her. He cried out as his cock slipped out of her tight warmth to be replaced in seconds by her hot mouth.

He was panting as she sucked and licked his length while her fist tightly circled his cock and pumped near the base, and her other hand lightly massaged his balls. His eyes rolled back in his head.

"Good God, Karen. You're the most amazing woman I've ever met. You win...I have to come. I can't hold it any longer. Let me be inside you though...in my fantasies I've always come while taking you from behind so I could come on your luscious ass."

Karen looked up and was stunned by what she saw in his eyes. It wasn't lust or need. It was warmth and desire and more. She reached up and cupping his cheek, leaned in to kiss him. It was a kiss filled with awe and wonder. She let her mouth move to his ear where she whispered "Fulfill your fantasies Nicholas, for they're mine too."

He wasted no time turning her around and sliding his hard length into her. His hands alternated between rough kneading and feather light touches on her ass.

"You have the most beautiful ass I've ever seen. It's perfection."

Karen thought to herself that the guy must be a bit insane to admire her fat ass, but in truth she didn't care. All she cared about was the feeling of him filling her.

"I love your thick, strong thighs…I've thought about them since the first minute I laid eyes on you. I wanted to grind my core against your leg and leave my scent all over you."

Nicholas cried out, "Fuck yes, Karen…I'm going to come."

He pumped his hips in a frenzied motion and Karen felt her climax hit her hard. Wave after wave swept through her, and she cried out with her intense pleasure.

Nicholas thrust with each spurt and then slid out, and Karen felt his hot cream hit her ass and back. He replaced his cock with two fingers as they rode out their orgasms.

Karen collapsed but Nicholas wasn't done. He used his cock to spread his come along Karen's crack. He slid his cock back and forth in the slick moisture.

"Mmmmm love…you feel so good, so slick and satiny against my cock."

His words and the feel of him sliding back and forth against her ass made her heartbeat accelerate. His scent enveloped her in a cocoon of desire.

Her hips started to move of their own accord. She wanted...she didn't know what she wanted, but she couldn't stop the feeling of need that came over her. She heard herself pleading "Please...I need—"

Nicholas soothed her. "I'm here for you love. I'll take care of you."

He spread her cheeks apart and rubbed his come around her opening.

"Has anyone ever taken you here before?" He softly asked her.

"No...never...."

He sucked in a breath. "I'm glad that I'll be the first." He leaned down and kissed the back of her head.

Karen moaned when she felt the broad head of his cock penetrate her. When he pushed in a little more she heard his moans join hers.

"Are you okay?" He asked with a voice that was hoarse.

"Yes...I want more," she moaned.

God help him, he wanted to slam into her, but he held back.

"Okay love...give me a minute to get control. You're so tight I...Ahhhhh...!"

With a cry she pushed back into him and his cock slid all the way into her.

"Karen...fuck...are you okay?" He rasped, even as his hips began to pump.

"Yeah...shut up and fuck me," she moaned.

With a cry, he took hold of her hips and fucked her with all he had. He came hard. He had no control as it spilled out. All he could do was groan with each spurt as he filled her with his seed.

They both lay there for minutes, trying to come back to themselves. Karen was the first to speak. "I guess this proves you're not impotent, and more importantly, that you will survive."

Nicholas was quiet for a moment and then said, "Yeah...about that...."

Chapter 23

Nicholas wanted to be anywhere in the world but here, staring into this amazing woman's eyes and telling her he had lied in order for them to escape. What just passed between them had changed everything, at least for him. He knew it was fucking crazy, but he loved her. He knew he shouldn't, but he did. While he was moving inside her it hit him. She was his match in every way: a strong leader, a passionate lover, and a lost soul. He couldn't continue to lie. He wanted to take her along with him when he left here, and he couldn't do that without the truth. He prayed that he wasn't making a mistake in trusting her, because it wasn't just his life, but the lives of seven other vampires at stake.

She stared at him expectantly.

"I lied. Vampires don't need sex to stay alive during the polar nights. It will kill us though. That much is true. It's due, in fact, to the way our organs process and use the blood we drink. If we don't sleep the organs can't optimize the blood and will eventually shut down."

Not looking at her he stood and sat on the end of the bed with his shoulders slumped.

"The others looked to me to help them escape that fate. I thought if we brought in women and seduced them and made them fall for us, they would be willing to help us escape. I tried to come up with other plans, but nothing else would work. This was the only way. I couldn't stand the look in Soren's eyes. His brother died here last year during the polar nights, and his were the only eyes that didn't hold dread thinking about what was about to befall us. His eyes held anticipation, and it hit me that he had gotten caught by UGA on purpose. He wanted to die, and I became enraged that just because we are different we should be condemned to death and be happy to do so. That's when I resolved to do whatever was necessary to free us all."

Nicholas stopped talking and closed his eyes, the silence telling him everything. He had lost. And worse, he had failed the others who would now die a slow and agonizing death because he fell in fucking love. How pathetic was that?

So wrapped up in his misery, he didn't hear her approach. He jumped when he felt her hands cup his face. She knelt in front of him with tears in her eyes.

"I didn't know. I didn't know about vampires. I didn't know they love and they suffer just like us. I'm so sorry…please forgive me."

Nicholas didn't move. He was in shock. He had lied and tricked her, and she was asking for his forgiveness?

"I understand if you can't forgive me, but at least give me a chance to make it right. I can help you all get out of here."

Nicholas kissed her. "I'm the one who's sorry. I should never have let these women be used like this. You may never believe this, but I am a gentleman."

She smiled and his insides melted. "You're right, I don't believe you. A gentleman would never fuck me hard against the wall."

Nicholas felt a sharp stab of desire hit his gut. Quietly he said, "I want to fuck you hard everywhere. In the shower, on your desk, in a car, in a dark alley, in an elevator, on a rooftop, in a crowded theater, and right here, right now on this bed."

Karen's thick voice muttered, "Holy shit."

"Holy shit, indeed. Even though I just came twice, I'm hard for you again." His eyes bored into hers. "A lifetime wouldn't be enough with you."

She swallowed hard and cleared her throat. "We better make some plans to get you out of here."

He let her change the subject because she was clearly uncomfortable with the depth of his feelings for her. He would give her time. The time it took for them to bust out of there, because he wasn't leaving without her.

An hour later Nicholas was knocking on the other vampires' doors to tell them to meet in his quarters in half an hour, and to leave the women in their rooms.

As the men filed into his room they looked at Karen sitting on a chair in the corner and gave him a questioning look. No doubt they were baffled to see him consorting with the enemy.

When the last one entered and shut the door, he began. "You can forget abort the plan with the women. We have another way to escape."

The men looked at Karen and then him sharply.

"It's okay. Karen is going to help us. Tomorrow night at 6 pm there will be a helicopter here to take us to an airstrip in Frankfurt. From there we will travel by plane to my island in Greece, where we can lay low for awhile before you all make your way to your respective homes."

Eduardo was the first to speak. "And we're to believe that they will just let us walk out of here?"

Jake piped in, "It sounds like an ambush to me."

The others agreed. Only Soren kept quiet.

Nicholas could understand their disbelief. "Karen is going to arrange for a power interruption at the same time."

Blayze, always the skeptic, said, "And you believe her? I can't believe you, of all men, would let a quick fuck cloud your senses. She must have been one hell of a lay."

Nicholas's hands were around Blayze's throat in seconds. "Don't you fucking talk about her like that. I will kill you where you stand, Frenchman."

The other vampires tried to pull his hands from Blayze's throat with no success.

"Nicholas, let him go," Karen said as she put a hand on his arm.

He let the man drop to the ground and took Karen's hand as she smiled at him. He knew that the other vampires were staring at him, but he didn't care. He kept his gaze only on Karen.

She stood in front of a room full of vampires and began to talk. "I can understand why you don't trust me, but I didn't know. I never knew that vampires were no different than me. I will take the blame in that, but you all must look to yourselves too. You never told us anything. You never opened your mouths and told us that you didn't want to drain and kill all humans. We didn't know that all you wanted was to live and love and be loved in return. We were worried about a threat to mankind, when we should have been worried about exploring the things we have in common, like love for a brother."

Nicholas held his breath, but Soren remained quiet.

"I don't want to keep you here any longer, but I can't just let you go. If I did, Bryce would place me in the brig and stop you. So tomorrow at six, I will arrange for a power interruption, at which time all electronic doors will be unlocked. There is a manual override for the elevator that you will have to use. Nicholas has arranged for a private helicopter to pick you up."

Liam asked, "What about you, lass? Won't you be in trouble for helping us?"

Nicholas kept quiet. Karen was going to be on that helicopter with them regardless of what she thought.

"No, I'll be fine. I have everything arranged that it will look like exactly what it is, a break out. I will be here acting angry and calling out the bloodhounds."

She looked at Nicholas. "Only those in this room will know how I truly feel."

"I'm not leaving her."

All heads swiveled. Nicholas could swear he didn't say that out loud. He hadn't...it was Soren.

"I'm not leaving here without Sparkle." He stood.

Both Nicholas's and Karen's mouths dropped open. He tried to reason with him. "Soren, I'm not sure I understand. We don't need to use the women anymore. We have an alternative plan to get out of here."

"You don't understand. I'm taking Sparkle with me. I can't leave here without her."

"Be reasonable...the others...." Nicholas looked around the room at the other men. None of them would meet his eyes.

He walked over to Jake. "Jake? What's going on?"

Jake looked at him. "Well, I want to take Nette too. She's rocked my world, Nicholas. I've never met anyone like her. She does things with whipped cream that you can only —"

"Enough!" Nicholas cut him off. He didn't want to hear the rest, and goddamn him! If he couldn't get the picture out of his mind of Jake wearing whipped cream, he was going to vomit.

He stood in front of Garrett.

"Yeah man...I can't leave Tamika. She needs me. I've started training her. Already her muscle mass has increased. I can't wait until she's as strong as me and whups my —"

Nicholas held up his hand and Garrett shut up.

Tor didn't wait for Nicholas to come over to him, he blurted out, "I'm taking Juls along too. My penis fits in her perfectly."

Nicholas shook his head. What the fuck was he supposed to say to that?

Eduardo was next. "Well amigos, I'm taking my Samantha too. She has taught me many sexual things. Did you know that a woman likes to have their cunt licked?"

Eduardo looked around at the other men, nodding his head as if he just revealed a great secret. No one looked back, afraid he would see their smirks.

Nicholas looked at Liam and crossed his arms, waiting for him to to say something that would creep him out. He wasn't disappointed.

"Ummm yeah...I want to take Barbara home with me." His eyes glazed over and he said, "I can't wait to play catch the milkmaid with her and spank her bare ass in my hayloft."

"For the love of God," Nicholas muttered. He turned and looked at Blayze. This was one vampire who would not have fallen for a human woman.

"I turned Diane into vampire," he said with no remorse.

The room erupted into shouts. The others were furious. Turning someone into vampire was serious. A lot didn't survive the transition.

"What the fuck were you thinking, Frenchman? You could have killed her!" Nicholas held his clenched fists at his side, ready to pummel his snotty ass.

Karen stepped between the two. She first looked at Nicholas. "Back down, Nicholas. The important thing is that Diane is all right." She looked at Blayze. "She is all right, isn't she?"

Blayze looked at Karen and actually gave her a small smile. "She is better than fine."

Karen smiled at him and mouthed "thank you" so that only he could see it. Blayze lifted her hand to his mouth and whispered, "No, thank you."

Nicholas did hear that and pulled Karen's hand back. "What's going on?"

"Nothing," both Karen and Blayze said in unison.

Karen turned and addressed the vampires once again. "All right, you say you want to keep the women. I say I want to hear the women say they want to keep you. Go back to your quarters and send the women to me. I have to be sure."

They left and Nicholas took her in his arms "Will you stay the night with me?"

She rubbed against his erection and laughed at his hiss. "It looks like I'll have to, unless you want Holly to try and help you with that."

"You're mean...you know I can't come unless I'm with you or thinking about you."

She asked him, "Why didn't you just try and picture me when you were with her?"

"Hell...that's the first time a woman ever asked me that. To be honest, I couldn't. I found touching her was like touching a dead fish. It was a little repugnant. All I wanted was you. So I bit her every night to drain her and make her pass out."

"You are bad." She playfully swiped at him and he hauled her back against him and kissed her. "I think they're coming back. I heard something."

He continued kissing her. "The hell with them." He pulled away and narrowed his eyes. "Why weren't you upset about Diane being turned vampire? And what was all that 'thank you' shit between you and Blayze?"

"Are you jealous?" She teased him.

"Hell yeah...I don't trust that Frenchman."

"I do. He saved Diane's life." Tears came to her eyes as she continued. "She was sick. She was sick before and just found out it returned."

Nicholas shook his head. Who knew the fucking Frenchman actually was a decent man?

He kissed Karen's hair. "I'm glad he turned her. He must care about her a lot to have made such a tough decision."

Just then the door opened, and the women came in, with the exception of Diane who was still weak from her transition.

Karen looked at them. She had a sense of déjà-vu. Was it only a few days ago she stood here greeting them and thanking them for their dedication to UGA? They were still the same strong, determined women they were a few days ago, and couldn't agree more when Nicholas leaned down and said into her ear. "We never stood a chance, did we?"

Smiling, she shook her head. He had no idea.

"Here we are again, but this time with a different goal before us. Now that you've gotten to know these vampires, I'm sure that like me, your whole mindset has been changed. We know these men are not just vampires, but men like your father or your brother."

Nette, who was never one to keep quiet, shouted out, "Whoa...I've never covered my brother's nipples in whipped cream."

Everyone laughed except Nicholas. "Not again with the whipped cream. Now the image is burned into my mind." He groaned.

Karen was surprised when Sparkle stepped forward.

"Karen, what is this about? I want to go back to Soren."

Well, that answered Karen's question. "I've decided to help the men escape. None of them want to leave without you. Although I will do my best to minimize the risk, something could go wrong. It's up to you if you want to stay or leave."

Karen and Nicholas held their breath.

Tamika went first. "I'm in. I'm crazy about Garrett."

"I love Liam," Barbara said softly.

Samantha came next. "Eduardo needs me. I'm in."

"Tor drives me crazy...I want to be with him," Juls said with a wink.

Nette said, "I'm in." And as if she was confessing a sin, "I'm in love with Jake."

Karen looked at Sparkle. She went to her and put her hands on Sparkle's shoulders. She was so young to have to make such a big decision.

Sparkle said in her quiet voice, "I'm going with Soren. He needs me."

Nicholas came over to stand before her. "Don't do it to protect Soren, do it because you want him."

"I need him too. He sees beyond the brain. No one has ever wanted or needed anything else from me. Only he can turn me from geeky girl to a desired woman."

Nicholas doubted that. Most men were fools when it came to women and their looks. He looked at the women before him and thought how they had paired off. No doubt the men thought they were getting exactly what they wanted, but they didn't. They got exactly what they needed. He was overwhelmed by this group of women. "You are an amazing group of women, and you honor us by helping us and loving us."

"Damn straight!" Nette shouted.

Karen watched as the women left. They were an amazing bunch of women. She was humbled by their good hearts.

Nicholas wrapped his arms around her. She turned in his arms and kissed him with desperation, because she knew this would be the last time they would be together.

Chapter 24

Nicholas had a bad feeling that had started when Karen left his bed early that morning. She looked so sad as she kissed him before she left. It was if she was saying goodbye.

He looked around the common room where they were all gathered. They were keyed up and ready to put the plan into action. Even Diane was up and looking almost normal. Only a vampire would be able to tell the effort she was putting forth to control her new vampire attributes.

They had a little less than an hour to wait. At 6 pm Karen would activate an alarm in her office to bring most of the guards running in her direction. A few minutes later she had a planned electrical failure scheduled via computer. As soon as the lights went out, the vampires were going to lead the women towards the elevator that would take them to the seed level of the vault, where they'd make their way to the outer door.

"Mother Fucker!" Nicholas swore loudly, jumping from his chair. Everyone in the room went silent. Nicholas pounded on the locked door to get the guards attention. When the guard pressed the button for the intercom he said. "I've got to see the commander. Now!"

The guard said, "The commander is busy —"

Nicholas yelled into the intercom, "Call her and tell her I said it's an emergency."

The guard picked up a phone. Thank God, Nicholas thought.

Soren was at his side. "What's going on, Nicholas?"

"She lied. Karen lied to us."

There were gasps from everyone in the room.

Blayze's eyes flashed. "She betrayed us?"

Sparkle shook her head. "I don't believe it. I won't believe it."

Nicholas turned toward the woman who stood up for Karen. "You're right. She didn't betray you. She betrayed me. She never planned to join us. She can't. She's planning to sacrifice herself so we can escape. The outer door can't be opened or overridden by a computer program. It can only be opened by activating a switch in the control room."

"How do you know this?" Soren asked.

He looked at the people in the room. "I'm one of the people who funded the Seed Vault Project. How fucking ironic is that?"

The guard came back like he was going to open the door when the alarm sounded.

"NO! NO!" Nicholas yelled. "Damn you, Karen."

The lights went out and the doors slid open with a "swoosh."

"Let's go!" Blayze shouted.

The vampires led the women out, having no problem seeing in the dark. Soren grabbed Nicholas's arm with the hand that wasn't clutching Sparkle.

"Nicholas, we have to go now."

Nicholas shrugged his hand off. "You go. Make sure everyone's safe. I'm going to get Karen."

Soren turned to Sparkle. "Go with Nette and Jake. I'm going to help Nicholas."

Nicholas stopped Sparkle from leaving. "No, you're not. You're going to take charge and get everyone safely on that helicopter."

Soren looked like he wanted to argue, but Nicholas gave him no chance as he took off in the direction of Karen's office.

Stubborn, stupid woman, he thought as he ran. She was also brave, loyal, and so filled with love that it humbled him. He didn't deserve such goodness.

He burst into her office and stopped dead. She had Holly in a head lock and was banging her head against the desk.

"And this is for having Nicholas's fingers inside you, and this is for your skanky blood that he had to ingest, and this one...." She banged Holly's head really hard on the desk and watched as she sank to the floor. "Is because I don't like your skinny ass."

Nicholas had leaned against the doorframe as he watched Karen beat the shit out of Holly, and had never been so turned on.

"My God, that made me hard."

Karen's head turned in his direction. She couldn't see him clearly as her flashlight had rolled into the corner during her scuffle.

"Nicholas! What are you doing here?" she asked as she scrambled towards the flashlight.

He sauntered towards her. "The better question is what are *you* doing here? And why were you beating Holly's head against the desk? Not that I disapprove, but that's a little much for a couple of quick orgasms."

"She's working with that piece of shit, Bryce. She overheard our whole plan because she was listening outside your quarters when we were making our plans. It was probably why she went after you in the first place."

"Ouch! That hurt."

"Oh! Stop your joking. You need to get out of here."

"I can't believe you lied to me, Karen."

Karen winced at the hurt in his voice. "It's the only way. I'll be okay. You have to go now."

"No."

"You have to. I need to go open the door for the others."

"Karen, I'm not leaving here without you. If you stay then I stay. You have to know that I'm in love with you."

"Oh Nicholas…I lo—"

"Well, well…isn't this sweet, two lovers being torn apart? So sad."

Bryce entered by a side door that Karen hadn't even known existed, and as Nicholas made a move towards him, he grabbed Karen and pointed a gun at her head.

"I don't think so, Vampire. If you make another move I'll blow your fucking whore's head off. Really Karen, if you were so desperate for a good fuck you could have asked me. I've always thought you were attractive: a little bit heavy in the caboose, but otherwise very fuckable."

Nicholas swore and looked like he was going to tear Bryce's head off.

"Don't worry, Nicholas. I accidentally saw him naked in the locker room once, and his cock is smaller than a Vienna sausage. There's no way he could give anyone a good fuck."

"You lying fucking bitch!" He screamed as he backhanded Karen and sent her flying.

Nicholas roared, "You're a dead man, you little motherfucker!"

He launched himself at Bryce as Karen struggled to her feet. She couldn't see anything.

Her heart stopped when she heard a shot.

"NICHOLAS? Oh God...please...." She crawled on the floor and picked up the flashlight. She started shaking when she saw Nicholas and Bryce lying on the floor in a strange embrace. She pushed Nicholas off and saw the bloodstain on his shirt.

"No...dear God...no."

She felt for a pulse and found a weak one. She spared a quick glance at Bryce and saw with no remorse that his neck had been snapped. She needed to get Nicholas topside fast so the other vampires could help him.

She picked up Bryce's gun and ran down the hall to the medical lab to get a stretcher. She wasn't sure how she would get Nicholas on it, but dammit, she would find a way.

She heard a noise from under the counter. Swinging the flashlight she saw the chief medical advisor cowering there like a scared rabbit. Just the help I need, she thought. She pointed the gun at him. "Come out of there, Mr. Sutter."

He crawled out with his shaking hands in the air.

"Oh for Christ's sake, put your hands down."

"Commander?"

"Yes. It's your commander. Come with me, I need your help."

He followed her back to her office and when she said, "Help me get him on the stretcher," he automatically went to help Bryce.

"Not him, you jackass. He's dead. He doesn't need any help."

"You want to help the vampire? I won't do it," he said, and stood to leave.

"Oh yes you will, because I have a gun, and so help me God I will shoot your sorry ass if you don't."

He gave her a hard glare. "You will go to prison for this."

"Oh well, three squares a day and no taxes. No biggie. Now get moving, because if he dies then so do you."

Karen watched as he put Nicholas on the stretcher. She walked behind him as they moved towards the elevator. When the elevator doors opened on the upper level, Tor and Garrett were there holding lead pipes, ready to knock some heads off.

Karen jumped out. "It's okay guys. It's me. I have Nicholas with me. He's hurt."

Eduardo moved forward. "He has a pulse...it's weak, but it's steady. He needs blood. We can give him some in the chopper."

"Go. Take him. I'll go open the door." Karen moved to press the button when Soren stopped her hand.

"Come with us. He'll kill us all for leaving you behind."

Karen smiled through her tears. "Nah...he'll be glad to be rid of my fat ass."

Soren looked sad and turned to leave.

"Soren?"

"Yes?"

"Tell him...tell him that I...." She looked at Soren, not able to say the words out loud.

"Don't worry Karen. I'll tell him." He nodded and the doors closed.

Sutter stood in the corner giving her a dirty look. She didn't care. She didn't care about anything. She just wanted to push the button to open the door to this damned seed vault, so that the man she loved could be free.

Chapter 25

Karen wiped the sweat from her brow. The boiling pots of water spewed a constant stream of steam. She opened a large box of spaghetti and dropped it into the boiling water. She hated kitchen duty. In the month since she'd been incarcerated in Louisiana State Prison she'd had kitchen duty twice. It was better than laundry duty, she supposed. It was hot down there too, but you also got headaches from the chemical detergent they used in large quantities.

Karen stirred the spaghetti with a large steel spoon. Things could have gone worse for Karen. The top dogs at UGA had gone easy on her due to her years of service. They could have easily sent her to Leavenworth for life if they'd wanted to. Instead, she got sent here for four to six years. Karen wasn't sorry she'd helped Nicholas and the others. She would do it again in a minute. Her daydreams about Nicholas were what got her through each day.

CRACK! Karen yelped as a spoon came down on the top of her head.

"Pay attention to what you're doing!" The head cook yelled at her.

Karen rubbed her head where a bump was already forming. She really needed to stop daydreaming during work. She would save that for when she was in her bunk and she could let her mind wander to the way Nicholas had held her and kissed her. She shook her head to clear it. For now she needed to concentrate on cooking spaghetti for four hundred of her closest friends.

That night as Karen lay on her bunk under the scratchy covers she thought about Nicholas. She smiled in the dark as she remembered how his hands had grabbed and caressed her ass. Karen found herself drifting in her pleasant memories and found peace. At least until the woman in the bunk below her pushed her foot against Karen.

"Karen, are you listening to me?"

Karen groaned. "No. I'm not listening to you, Betsy."

Karen had listened enough to Betsy. Betsy talked all the time. She had an opinion on everything from the nutritional value of the meals that were served to them to her opinion and answers for global warming.

As usual Betsy ignored Karen and went on talking. "I was telling you about the new guard they hired for the night shift on C block. He's gorgeous. The women over there have been playing with themselves non-stop since he started."

"Can they hire a male guard? That doesn't seem right."

At Karen's question Betsy really became animated. "Every so often they hire one. Especially when the warden meets a man she wants to fuck. She'll tell the state board she's in dire need and that there aren't any other female candidates available. She's in dire need all right." Betsy cackled.

That's not right, Karen thought. That woman was using her power to get a piece of ass? Bitch!

Karen tried to get back to her daydreams of Nicholas, but now that Betsy was finally quiet, the guard's footsteps were echoing down the hall. She heard them stop in front of her cell. She waited to move until the guard left. The middle shift guard could be a cruel bitch, and was known for roughing up some of the girls.

Karen's breath caught when she heard a key turning. Karen closed her eyes. She didn't want to see poor Betsy beaten. Betsy was annoying, but she was also mentally challenged and it just wasn't fucking fair.

Without turning Karen said quietly, "Don't hurt Betsy. I'll go with you."

Karen's heart stopped beating when she heard a familiar voice say, "I heard that people who are incarcerated need to have sex so they don't die."

Karen flew off the bunk and slammed into Nicholas's chest. He caught her in his arms.

"Oh baby, I missed you. Are you okay?"

Karen laughed. "Am I okay? Are you okay? The last I saw you were bleeding from a gunshot wound. I've been so worried."

Nicholas closed his eyes. "You've gone to prison for helping me and you're worried about me? Karen, you've got to be kidding. You're one of the mo—"

"Aren't you going to kiss her?"

Nicholas and Karen turned to stare at Betsy, who was sitting on the edge of her bed, smiling and clapping her hands.

"You better believe I'm going to kiss her." And he did. He broke away reluctantly. "We have to go. We don't have much time."

He pulled Karen towards the door.

"Wait…Betsy?" She said, and looked at him with those big hazel eyes.

He sighed. He couldn't deny her anything. "Come along Betsy, but be quiet. We're going on a little trip."

Karen smiled and let him lead the way. She was nervous at every corner they took that a guard would pop out and stop them, and she almost screamed when a guard appeared in front of them.

Nicholas quickly said, "It's okay. It's Diane."

Karen looked closer and indeed it was Diane. She had dyed her hair blonde and was wearing glasses. Karen hugged her fiercely.

"I can't believe it's you. You look wonderful."

Diane smiled. "Thanks to you."

"If the two of you can hold off a while longer to have this reunion, we need to get moving."

They went down the hall and slipped into the laundry room where they were met by Blayze, who was wearing the white uniform of a deliveryman. He kissed Diane on the cheek and said, "Nice to see you again, Karen."

Karen was dumbfounded, but now wasn't the time to ask questions. Blayze opened a door that led to a laundry truck and they all climbed in the back. Blayze closed the doors with a quick wink.

Karen opened her mouth to ask Nicholas what was going on, but he held a finger over his lips. The truck started and they began a bumpy ride out of the prison. After a few minutes they stopped.

Karen heard Blayze speak with someone and she held her breath. All must have gone okay, because the truck started rolling again. Nicholas slid closer to her and took her hand in his. Karen's breath hitched when he lightly kissed her fingers.

Nicholas finally spoke. "We began making plans to break you out the minute we got to my island. Blayze has been working at this laundry company for the past three weeks."

Karen couldn't believe it.

Diane laughed. "Believe it. He may have missed his calling. He's been telling me that when he gets home he has to instruct his maid on the best way to remove blood stains from his clothing."

Karen and Diane laughed and hugged each other.

The truck rolled to a stop and the door was flung open. Diane jumped down first and helped Betsy, who was, for the first time in her life, in awe and strangely quiet. Then Nicholas jumped down with Karen in his arms and reluctantly set her down.

Karen hurried over to hug Blayze. "Thank you, Blayze."

Blayze looked over at Diane. "No, it's you who deserves the thanks."

"He's right you know." Karen gasped as Soren moved out from the side of the van.

Sparkle came next. "If it wasn't for you all of us wouldn't have found each other."

One by one they all came out, till eight vampires and nine women were gathered. Karen stood there crying.

"You all came for me, and Blayze worked in a *laundry* for me?"

She turned back to Nicholas. "You and Diane got guard jobs...?"

A thought came to Karen and her eyes narrowed at Nicholas. "Hey! What did you do to the warden to get a job in a woman's prison?"

Nicholas looked stern. "I would do anything to secure your freedom, and if that means giving my body to a woman who couldn't resist her raging desire for me, I would!"

Karen rolled her eyes. "You bit her, didn't you?"

"Yeah."

The End

About the Author

Jude Stephens is the author of several vampire novels. She also writes short story horror. When asked why she delves into the paranormal, she explains, "It's pretty simple. I like to be scared."

Early influences were Stephen King and Dean Koontz.

Jude lives in Eastern Pennsylvania and has two grown children Mark and Megan and a granddaughter. In her spare time she enjoys traveling with her fiancé Walter, one of their favorite cities is New Orleans. He likes the jazz and she likes the ghosts.

Jude is currently working on several sequels to some of her popular vampire series.